Extreme Pursuit

T0352251

ALSO BY ALEX KINGWELL

Extreme Exposure

Extreme Pursuit

ALEX KINGWELL

New York   Boston

Copyright © 2016 by Alex Kingwell
Excerpt from *Extreme Exposure* copyright © 2016 by Alex Kingwell
Cover design by Brian Lemus
Cover copyright © 2016 by Hachette Book Group, Inc.

Forever Yours
Hachette Book Group
1290 Avenue of the Americas
New York, NY 10104
hachettebookgroup.com
twitter.com/foreverromance

First edition: May 2016

Forever Yours is an imprint of Grand Central Publishing.
The Forever Yours name and logo are trademarks of Hachette Book Group, Inc.

The publisher is not responsible for websites (or their content) that are not owned by the publisher.

The Hachette Speakers Bureau provides a wide range of authors for speaking events. To find out more, go to www.hachettespeakersbureau.com or call (866) 376-6591.

ISBN 978-1-4555-6533-7 (ebook edition)
ISBN 978-1-4555-6534-4 (print on demand edition)

E3

As always, there are many people to thank—family, friends, and the team at Forever Yours—but an extra note of gratitude goes to Selina McLemore for her insightful editorial guidance.

Extreme Pursuit

CHAPTER ONE

Nicky Bosko didn't see the beat cop until it was too late. She was thirty steps from the intersection, and he was tucked in around the corner, his eyes tracking a homeless man pushing a shopping cart down the rain-slicked sidewalk.

Her heart constricted, as if someone had reached in and grabbed it. The girl walking beside Nicky followed her gaze, froze.

Nicky grabbed the girl's arm. "Keep walking." She pitched her voice low.

They had no choice. A cold drizzle had emptied the sidewalks, and the cop would notice them for sure if they turned back or tried to cross the street. They had to keep going and pass by him.

The girl had that deer-in-the-headlights look, her eyes wide as saucers. "He'll see me." The words seemed to catch in her throat.

"No, he won't." Nicky tried to sound confident even as her stomach twisted into a hard knot.

The cop, his hands hooked behind his back, was ruddy faced, stout, and he wore a dark rain jacket. He stood under an awning, partially protected from the rain, which a west wind drove down at a slant toward him.

The homeless guy stopped to peer into a steel mesh garbage can, parking his cart at an angle that blocked the sidewalk.

Stuck behind him, the knot in Nicky's gut tightened. Forcing herself not to look at the cop, she focused on the homeless guy. Fat raindrops slid down the green garbage bag he wore as a poncho. He had frizzy gray hair that flared out from under a navy beanie, reaching his shoulders.

The girl's eyes darted around, as if looking for an escape route. Nicky tightened her grip on her arm as the homeless man finished inspecting the garbage can. Straightening, he wheeled the cart to the left, having decided to take the cross street. He waited at the curb for a green pedestrian signal.

Nicky and the girl kept going straight ahead. Just as they reached the curb, the pedestrian light flashed yellow. She bit the inside of her cheek, cursed under her breath. Cars and buses cruised by, their tires hissing on the wet road and spitting up water. Wiping rain from her forehead, she glanced to the right, past the cop and up the side street. Dark clouds hung low in the bleak sky. On the other side of the drugstore was an office building, then a four-story car park. On the next block, a patrol car pulled to the side of the road. Nicky held her breath until two officers got out, walked into a building.

There were two ways this could go. They could run now, in any direction. The cop'd call for help, give chase, and chances were one or both of them would be caught, possibly before they got farther than a block or two.

Or they could keep walking. Hope the cop didn't recognize the girl. She wore Nicky's navy blue rain jacket and a ball cap pulled down low over her forehead, but her picture was everywhere and, since her father was a cop, there'd be extra incentive to catch this runaway. A vivid memory surfaced, something Nicky hadn't thought about in months, and her stomach clenched. She'd been fourteen, a terrified runaway huddled on a New York sidewalk, scavenging in garbage cans for food. But she'd been lucky. A female cop had taken her to a shelter. That wouldn't happen with Michelle. This cop, any cop, would deliver her back to her father.

But she had to keep her cool. If the cop recognized her, they'd run then.

She shot another glance at the girl. Her name was Michelle Stafford and she was five foot six, almost Nicky's height, thirteen years old. Her soft, tiny facial features were still that of a child, but a somber guardedness in those gray-blue eyes suggested she'd already witnessed too much of life's dark side. That and the large bruise yellowing on her left cheek.

Nicky tightened her fists as a sudden fierce resolve coursed through her. She felt like a mama bear protecting her cub. The cops wouldn't get Michelle, not if she could help it.

Four people now waited with them to cross the street. She snuck a glance back at the cop. He caught her eye, gave her the once-over. Looking away, she sucked in a ragged breath. Caught a whiff of wet cement, which somehow reminded her of running track in high school. Practicing sprints and hurdles in the chill fall air. She'd been fast, probably still was. The girl would be, too.

The cop didn't look fast. But maybe he wouldn't need to be.

Holding her breath, waiting for him to shout at them to stop, she kept him in her peripheral vision, ready to run if he moved a single step.

A car honked its horn. She jumped, swallowed hard. Beside her, a woman in hospital scrubs spoke loudly into a cell phone. Somebody had botched the grooming of her dog. Coco now had an eye infection and the woman wanted everybody in Riverton in on that little tidbit. Across the street, a woman in red running shorts bounced up and down on her toes, impatient to cross.

Michelle didn't say anything, just stood, her body rigid, stared straight ahead.

At last the light changed. Starting across the intersection, Nicky kept a steadying hand on the girl's arm and forced herself not to hurry, to go with the flow. Not until they were on the other side of the street did she let out a heavy breath.

A tear escaped Michelle's eye and slipped down the middle of her bruised cheek. Nicky squeezed her hand. "Just a couple more blocks, Michelle. You'll be okay."

She scanned the sidewalk. A young guy in an acid-wash jean jacket and baggy pants stared at her as he walked toward them. He wasn't looking at Michelle, but Nicky kept her eye on him until they passed. Paranoia strikes deep.

Michelle had arrived at the shelter last week, brought in by another kid after two nights on the streets. This morning, they'd convinced her to see a doctor. Nicky thought about what the doctor had told her after, while Michelle used the bathroom. Her throat soured. No wonder she'd run away. But that was a whole other worry.

A block from the shelter, the sun broke through the low clouds, flashed off car windshields. More people spilled onto the sidewalks. That was good and bad. She and Michelle weren't as exposed, but it'd be harder to tell if they were being followed. Not that she had any skills on that front. She was a youth worker, not some covert operator.

Her eyes swept the length of the street, taking in the four people in a bus shelter up ahead and, just past them, a woman in a tight cobalt-blue dress and five-inch heels leaning against a door, smoking a cigarette. Across the road, a man walking a muscular dog stopped to read a menu posted outside a new pizzeria. Cars streamed by. Nobody slowed or seemed to take any interest in them.

Rolling her shoulders, she tried to shake off some of the tension. She felt sweaty despite the September chill and her damp hair and clothes.

The cigarette smoker ground the butt into the sidewalk with the toe of her shoe, smoothed her dress, and then vanished inside a shoe shop.

Nicky pointed out a department store just past the shoe shop. "They have a section for teens upstairs. We could go check it out if you'd like."

The girl brightened. "Oh, please. I hardly have any clothes." Her voice was soft, surprisingly low-pitched. "One of the girls loaned me a T-shirt and a pair of jeans, but they're too big."

Nicky smiled. Those were the most words the girl had strung together in two days. It'd been hard to tell if she was naturally quiet or had switched off because of everything she'd been through.

Five minutes later, they turned the final corner before the youth shelter. The tan brick building was on the other side of the street, down half a block. Out front, in a no-parking zone, a man leaned against a dark gray sedan. Tall and broad-shouldered, he wore a light shirt and dark pants.

Nicky stopped short. Something needled at the edge of her brain, made the hairs stand up on the back of her neck. It took a second more to process what it was. No kids were outside, hanging out in the sunshine on the front steps.

The man was a cop.

Her heart pounding against her ribs, she grabbed Michelle's arm. The girl looked at her, tilted her head to the side. Nicky nodded in the direction of the shelter. "See that man beside the car? I think he's a cop." She reached into her shoulder bag, fished out her cell phone, and shoved it into Michelle's hand.

The man looked in their direction. Seeing them, he uncrossed his arms, pushed himself away from the car, pulled out his wallet, and flashed a badge.

Nicky said, "Call the shelter in an hour. The number's programmed in there." Her eyes searched the girl's face. "Promise?"

Michelle glanced at the man, back at Nicky. Clasping the cell phone, she nodded. Already she was up on the balls of her feet, just waiting for the go-ahead.

Nicky said, "Remember that department store? Go in there. There's an exit at the back to the next street over." She pressed some bills from her wallet into the girl's hand. "Hide out for a couple of hours, then phone. Don't use your own phone. Okay?"

Michelle's lips trembled and her eyes bounced from the cop, who stood by his car, watching them, swinging his arms, back to Nicky. "Okay."

Michelle turned, bolted up the street. She slowed for a second to hook the knapsack on both shoulders but didn't look back. She was fast, all right. Her long legs flew over the pavement.

Nicky turned back to the cop. He was halfway across the street, a hand outstretched to stop cars. His mouth was open in surprise, his eyes locked onto Nicky.

A glance up the street showed that Michelle had disappeared. She just had to stall the cop, to ensure Michelle got away. It didn't look like he had called for help, which gave Michelle at least a fighting chance.

Across the street now, the cop started walking quickly down the sidewalk toward her, his bearing that of a man more used to giving orders than receiving them. Even from fifty yards she could tell he was a looker. Dark blond hair, striking, sharp facial features. And big, with a broad, muscular chest, and plenty through the arms and shoulders. At least a head taller than her. The word "strapping" came to mind.

An urge to run came upon her but she stood her ground. Foolhardy she could be but never cowardly.

The cop's approach caught the attention of a middle-aged

man in a suit walking past her. Slowing to catch the action, the suit looked from Nicky to the cop and back at her again. A hard stare convinced him to move on.

The cop stopped in front of her, flashed a shiny metal badge in her face. "Police Investigator," it said. Her glance moved up his chest—lingering momentarily on the man cleavage peeking out from two undone buttons—to his face. He was hot, all right. Off-the-charts hot, with impressive eyebrows, a strong jaw, and a long, straight nose on a squarish face. His hair was messy and in need of a trim but, combined with the stubble on his chin, gave an impression of rough, raw masculinity more in keeping with thugs than cops. He'd be a natural at undercover work.

She met his eyes, felt her mouth drop open.

They were intense.

It wasn't just their color—a clear, medium blue—but the way he was looking at her. But not in a way that suggested he liked what he saw. If anything, the opposite. More like the way a plastic surgeon might examine a particularly nasty facial disfigurement. A very rude plastic surgeon.

Swallowing hard, she took a full step back.

It was too weird. She said, "What are you looking at?"

He looked away for a moment, gave his head a little shake, then back at her. "You are Nicole Bosko?" His expression wasn't as intense now, and she had the feeling he was making an effort to tone it down.

There didn't seem any point in lying. She nodded, then gestured across the street toward the shelter. "I'm late for work."

He held up a hand. "I'm Detective Cullen Fraser. I have some questions I'd like to ask you."

"I'm sure you do, but I have no intention of answering them."

Those thick brows furrowed. "You don't even know what it's about."

The chambray shirt he was wearing brought out the color in those penetrating eyes. He would wear blue a lot—she'd bet good money on him being the vain type.

"Of course I know what it's about," she said, her irritation building. "Don't you have better things to do than harass innocent kids? It's not like they don't have enough problems without the cops coming down on them."

He crinkled his brow. "Drop the attitude, will you? I'm just trying to do my job."

She ground her teeth. "Unlike you, my job involves helping those kids. Some of them don't even have families." She thought about Michelle. "Or they'd be better off without their so-called families."

His lip curled. "Bad families, are you still blaming all your problems on that?"

She jerked back. What did her past have to do with this? Feeling her cheeks burn, she clenched her fists at her side. "You want to talk about *my* family?"

"Actually, yes, I do. What did you think I wanted to talk to you about?" He had his feet planted wide and his hands on his hips. "Have you done something illegal I should be aware of?"

"Of course not." She cleared her throat. "What is this about, then? Are my father and sister okay?"

"They're fine. It's concerning a cold-case investigation."

She eyed him warily. "Cold case? What cold case?" It was a trick; it had to be.

He cleared his throat. "I really don't want to talk about this in the middle of the street."

It was her turn to put her hands on her hips. "Too bad, because I'm not going anywhere with you until you tell me what's going on."

He cleared his throat. "It concerns your mother."

A sudden coldness squeezed her heart as more of her past slammed into the present. A long-buried past. She squeezed her eyes shut, willed her mind to go blank. Some memories, even painful, humiliating ones from her teen years, she could take. They reminded her of how far she'd come, and how easily things could go wrong. But Lisa Bosko? No way. No good would come of going down that road.

Already shock was giving way to anger. "My mother? I don't have a mother," she spat out. "And that means I have even more reason not to talk to you."

She brushed past him, stepped to the edge of the sidewalk, waited for a break in the traffic so she could cross.

"Don't you want to know what happened to her?"

His voice came from right behind her. She sucked in a deep breath, turned to face him, hating the weakness that was fanning a tiny flame of curiosity deep inside her. "Has she gone missing again? Is her new family looking for her?"

"It's not like that," he said flatly. Something dark flashed in his eyes.

Her heart pounding against her ribs, she stared at him. For the first time in years, her life was on track, an achievement made possible only after she'd packed up memories of Lisa Bosko and buried them in a deep, dark corner of her mind. Exhuming them would be stupid. Really stupid.

If she had any sense, she'd run as fast as she could in the other direction.

He watched her, lips pursed but not saying anything.

A sinking feeling hit the pit of her stomach. Good sense never had been her strong suit.

CHAPTER TWO

Cullen watched Nicole Bosko closely, tried to read her expression. Anger? Curiosity? It was impossible to tell.

"Well?" she said. "I'm listening. Tell me what happened."

Cullen shook his head. "I'd be happy to, but not here, in the middle of the street."

She was gorgeous, as he'd guessed she would be, tall and slim, with a perfect oval face framed by long brown hair, big brown eyes, and high cheekbones that hinted at Slavic ancestry. It was an easy beauty, the kind that might have been spoiled by too much makeup, but she wore little or maybe even none and seemed unaware of the effect of her looks.

Or maybe she was very much aware. Cullen had no idea. He was still spooked from seeing her in the flesh.

She said, "Why not? I promise not to get upset." A barely perceptible smile of contempt played on her full lips.

He gritted his teeth. His patience, already wire-taut, was about to snap. Sucking in a deep breath, he told himself to keep his cool. She seemed to want to piss him off. As if not giving a shit about her mother wasn't already accomplishing that goal.

He shook his head. "Come with me to the station. We'll talk there. I promise it won't take long."

She fingered a thin gold chain around her neck, and curiosity must have won her over, because she said, "All right, but I'll have to let them know at work I'm going to be late."

They walked across the street. He waited in the car while she went inside the shelter. Five minutes later, she came back out and got in the car. After she buckled up, he pulled into traffic.

At the station, she drew a few looks as they walked off the elevator and through the squad room. Not subtle, either. He led her down the hallway to his cramped office, where he gestured to a chair in front of his partner's desk, then went off to get his partner, Anna Ackerman.

When they returned, Anna introduced herself, then sat at her desk and sifted through some files to find the one she was looking for. He leaned against the front of Anna's desk, to the side so he didn't block Anna.

Bosko said, "Can you tell me what this is about now?" Her tone was clipped, impatient.

Anna said, "We'll get to that. We just have some routine questions for you first."

Bosko crossed her arms. "Fire away."

Anna said, "You're originally from Stephenville, just north of Riverton?"

"That's correct."

"You work at Stevens Youth Shelter?"

She narrowed her eyes. "I'm not going to talk about my work at the shelter, and especially about any of the kids I help. It's all confidential information, which I'm sure both of you know."

Anna shot him a questioning look. He said, "I already told you that this has nothing to do with the shelter. It's just for background information."

Bosko glared at him. "Yes, I work at the shelter, as you already know."

Anna said, "Tell me about your family."

Bosko stiffened, sat forward. "Your partner said they were okay. Are they?"

Anna said, "They're fine. Again, it's just background."

Bosko said, "I have a father, James, and a sister. Her name is Karina. She's five years older."

Anna said, "Your father's a doctor?"

A hard look signaled her impatience. "There you go again. Asking questions you already know the answers to. You may not know his specialty. He's a perinatologist. That's—"

"A specialty for high-risk pregnancies," Cullen cut in before she could explain. He leaned over, looked at a newspaper clipping. "I see your sister is a nurse. And a concert pianist. Very accomplished."

"You bet, Sherlock." She nodded at the clipping. "That's probably about her latest recording, the one of Bach concertos."

She played with her necklace again, and then her hand dropped to her lap. Her breasts, firm and round, molded to the thin fabric of her T-shirt. Swallowing hard, he looked away.

He said, "The local paper seems to like your sister. They give her a lot of publicity."

"It's her fresh-faced good looks. In Riverton, Karina's a superstar."

Looking at her Karina's picture, you could tell they were sisters. But Nicole had more of her mother's looks.

He said, "And you?"

"I'm not any kind of star. A chronic underachiever, as my father always said."

Anna read from a file. "You last saw your mother, Lisa Bosko, when you were five?"

Bosko's fingernails dug into the upholstered arms of her chair. She nodded. "If you're looking for her, I can't help you. She took off when I was five and I haven't seen her since."

Anna said, "You're sure about that?"

Bosko lifted her chin. "Of course I'm sure. She's most likely living quite happily somewhere with another family, unless she'd decided to ditch them, too."

Anna said, "We've read a transcript of an interview conducted with your father when your mother first went missing. There was apparently some suggestion that you had some behavioral problems that caused difficulty at home."

Bosko's eyes were cold. "Correct. Apparently I was too much to handle. I don't remember it myself, but I suppose I was too busy causing those problems."

Anna said, "Were you interviewed?"

"Again, I don't remember. I was five."

He cut in, "Have you ever tried to find your mother?"

"Why would I? She didn't want anything to do with me. As far as I know, she hasn't contacted my father, either. But you should ask him."

"That's going to be a bit of a challenge. Your father and sister have left the country."

"Left the country?" Surprise was evident in her tone.

"You didn't know?" Clearly, they weren't close. When she didn't say anything, he continued. "They're in Haiti, in a remote area on a relief mission. We've been trying to reach them, but the cell phone service is sketchy. They're not due back for another week."

She shrugged. "I can't help you there. We're not particularly tight, as you may have gathered. And I don't know anything about my mother."

Her eyes were dark, the color of deep mahogany, and spaced wide apart. Too wide apart, but they were balanced by a strong chin, and something about them suggested a sharp intelligence.

He said, "There's bitterness in your voice."

"You're imagining things. I'm not bitter at all. I used to resent my mother but she moved on and so did I. To tell you the truth, I hardly even think about Lisa Bosko now, and I certainly don't remember much." She glanced at her watch. "But please be careful about approaching my father. He had a heart attack last year. He shouldn't be bothered about this."

Anna shot Cullen a look, then said, "What do you remember about the day she left?"

She said, "I came home from school and she wasn't there. It was two decades ago. That's all I remember. Are you trying to find her again? Is that what this is about? Why don't you just tell me?"

He ignored her questions. "Did you see her leave?"

"No, I did not." She spoke slowly, emphasizing her words. "But everybody knew she wanted to leave."

"Why do you say that?"

"There was a note. Don't you have it?"

He said, "We've seen a copy."

Bosko put up her hands in mock surrender. "Sorry I couldn't be of more assistance." She stood up. "I have to get to work now. Good luck tracking her down."

He said, "We have something to show you before you go."

"I really don't care what you have to show me."

Ignoring her, he walked to a tall metal cabinet on the wall beside Anna's desk, opened the door. On the top shelf was a clay sculpture of a woman's head. Seeing it again, a chill ran down his spine.

Bosko glanced over. For a second, her expression didn't change. Then the color drained from her face. She looked from him to Anna, then walked slowly, as if in a trance, and stood in front of the cabinet. One shaky hand reached out to touch the sculpture but drew back. Glancing at him, a look of vulnerability and fear swept across her face. She said, "Why do you have a bust of me?"

He said, "You should sit down."

"I don't want to sit down. Tell me."

He said, "It's a facial reconstruction, but it's not you."

Her confusion was understandable. The bust looked so much like Nicole Bosko—the oval face, high cheekbones, wide-set eyes, small mouth—it was as if she'd posed for it. A few things were off, the face too fleshy, the nose too short.

"Then who is it?" Realization dawning, she covered her mouth and her eyes went wide.

"It's your mother," he said. "Your mother is dead."

CHAPTER THREE

Nicky clutched her chest, which felt heavy, as if crushed under a great weight. She couldn't breathe.

Squeezing her eyes shut, hiding her face in her hands, she tried to block it all out. Blood rushed in her ears like the din of a white noise. Then her legs felt wobbly and she stumbled. Strong arms encircled her shoulders, guided her to a chair.

When she opened her eyes again, reality slapped her in the face as her mother stared at her. She hadn't looked at a picture of her mother in a long time; over the years, Lisa Bosko's face had become darker and blurrier. But, her initial confusion aside, there was no question the sculpture was of her mother. It was so detailed, so real, the work an artist. An artist who had taken a lump of flesh-colored clay and molded it into something that was eerily lifelike.

Except there was no life. Her mother was dead.

She wanted to stop everything right now, to go back in time, run away and never have to face this awful truth. All those years she'd daydreamed of her mother having a happy life, secretly hating her, and it had been a fantasy. The truth was so much worse.

A new realization twisted her insides like a vise. Opening her eyes, looking at the reconstruction, it if was as if Nicky were gazing at herself. She'd even thought it was herself when she'd first seen it. Those were her eyes. Her lips. Her cheeks. People had told her she was a spitting image of her mother. Here was proof. It explained the look of shock on Fraser's face in the park.

Hot tears stinging the corners of her eyes, she hid her face, tried to slow her thundering heart. Her mother was dead.

A minute passed, maybe more. Acid rose in her stomach as her brain tried to process what this meant. She'd give anything now for her mother to be alive. It wouldn't matter if she had another family, if Nicky would never have the chance to see her again. If she could just be alive.

Her pulse took another kick. What about her father? This would kill him.

After several minutes, finally able to stop crying, she wiped a hand across her eyes and looked up. Ackerman picked up a glass of water off the desk and passed it to Nicky. Using both hands to steady the glass, she brought it to her mouth, swallowed a big gulp, and then snatched a tissue from a box Ackerman held out.

She had to get under control, be rational. Looking from one to the other, she said, "Tell me what this is all about."

Ackerman now stood in front of the desk, Fraser near the cabinet. She said, "I'm sorry to have to tell you this, Nicole, but your mother's remains were found three months ago."

More tears fell. "Where?" She fixated on the black eyeliner Ackerman wore on her top lids. That and thick mascara made her look harsh, although her manner wasn't. A short woman, somewhere in her forties and at least a decade older than Fraser, she was the good cop to his bad, it seemed.

"At an abandoned farm just across the border in New Hampshire."

Grabbing more tissues, she blew her nose. "You're sure it's my mother?" It came out more as a statement than a question. How could there be any doubt?

Ackerman nodded. "No identification was found with the remains. However, there was enough usable DNA from the skull. It's a long process, but that's how we tracked you down. You shared fifty percent of the dead woman's DNA, so we knew you were her daughter"

Fraser said, "Of course we had a bit of trouble finding you. Why'd you have the DNA test done?"

The question irked her. "It's not against the law, is it, to have your DNA mapped? People do it all the time to test for diseases."

"That doesn't answer the question."

His eyes looked assessing, betraying no sympathy. Some things you can't hide.

Nicky struggled to remain calm. "I took a genetics course last spring. A couple of us in the class decided to do it. I certainly didn't have any criminal intent."

Anna said, "So why did you use an assumed name? You said you were Nola Deveau."

"Because I didn't feel comfortable giving a private company access to my genetic information. And I don't like the fact that you now have it." She took another sip of water, her hands still shaky. "How did you find out it was me?"

Ackerman said, "When we realized Nola Deveau was fake, we knew the mother couldn't be identified until we had Nola's real identity. So we tracked you down. If we hadn't been successful, the image would have been released to the media."

Nicky rubbed her face in her hands. "You said the remains were found a month ago? Who found her body?"

"Three months," Ackerman said. "It was at an old farm in a little place near the border with New Hampshire called Lisette. It's being developed for a subdivision. Surveyors found her."

She shook her head, still reeling. "Lisette?" An image of an old house came to mind. It was fuzzy, just out of her grasp.

Ackerman said, "What is it?"

"I think I went there. With my mother."

"When?" Ackerman said.

"When I was little, I think my mom took me there."

"Just you and your mom?"

"Yeah, Karina was in school. My mother liked photography. It was a hobby. She liked taking pictures of abandoned buildings. I remember seeing an album of her photographs a few years back. My father must have kept them." More memories surfaced and she gave a small smile. "She never went anywhere without a camera. I do remember that about her."

Fraser, standing beside the cabinet, said, "Do you remember being in the town? Or at the farm?"

She considered this. "The farm. There was a big white house. It was falling down. There was some furniture still in the house. A sofa, a doll's carriage. I think there was a barn, or maybe it was a big shed."

"Did you ever meet anybody there?"

She shrugged. "I don't think so. I'm not even sure this place was in Lisette." She thought about it some more. "But I think I remember Mom talking about Lisette. It was close to her own name, Lisa."

Drying her eyes again, she felt their eyes on her. "I'm surprised she lived so close. I always figured she'd moved to the other side of the country, so nobody would recognize her."

Receiving no response, Nicky said, "Are you trying to locate her new family? Maybe they live near Lisette. Or maybe they just came for a visit."

Fraser said, "It's doubtful there was a new family."

Her stomach twisted. "What do you mean?"

He cleared his throat. "Her remains were there a long time. It's hard to say exactly how long, but it could be twenty years. The skeleton helped us determine the age."

The twist deep in her gut became a gnawing pain. "Twenty years? That can't be. Why wasn't her body found earlier?"

"The grave was fairly deep and it seems nobody had gone near the property for quite a few years. But it was sold recently and plans were made for the subdivision. Some excavation had begun."

Standing up, clutching her stomach, she walked over to the sculpture. Fraser took a step back to give her some space. Why hadn't she realized earlier? The reconstruction was of her mother when she was still young, maybe just a bit older than Nicky was now. The artist had scratched two faint lines across the forehead.

It was of her mother as she had looked when she'd gone missing.

An icy chill settled in her stomach. "Did she kill herself?"

Shaking his head, Fraser looked down. "She was murdered."

* * *

Cullen grabbed Nicole Bosko's arm. Her face had gone three shades whiter and she looked unsteady on her feet.

"You should sit down," he said.

Glancing at him, her nostrils flared. In the next instant she lunged at him and banged her fists on his chest. "Why didn't you just tell me? Why did you have to pull this charade?"

He grabbed her wrists, but she wrenched them free, then stepped back.

She looked from Anna back to him. "Did you think I had something to do with her death? For God's sake, I was five years old. I might have been a bad kid, but I wasn't *that* bad."

Anna said, "We're not suggesting that at all."

Bosko sat down, glared at them. "In a minute, I'm going to walk out of that door and I hope to never see either of you again." She clenched, then unclenched, her fists. "But first, you owe me an explanation. How did she die?"

He said, "There was evidence of a trauma to the skull."

She swallowed, grabbed a tissue to wipe her eyes, and then met his eyes. "Who did it?"

"We are trying to find that out."

"This happened about the time she disappeared?"

"Correct," Fraser said.

He could almost see the wheels in her head turning as she stared at the far wall. Clearing his throat, he waited for the next question.

Wet eyes met his again. "She didn't try to run away at all, did she?"

He pursed his lips, cleared his throat. "We are considering the possibility, yes."

* * *

"I've got ten minutes. Run me through this."

The police chief, Joan Mullen, had summoned Cullen and Anna to her office after they'd finished interviewing Nicole Bosko.

Anna said, "Lisa Marie Bosko was reported missing on a Saturday nineteen years ago this September. She was thirty-one. She'd apparently left a note saying she was going away. At the time it was a missing person case. There was a search but it turned up nothing."

"Why'd they search if she left a note?" Mullen's tone was brusque. In the job just three months, she'd quickly developed a reputation as a smart but hard-nosed boss. Cullen and Anna weren't the only cops hoping she'd loosen up after she'd been in the job a while.

Anna cleared her throat. "She was only supposed to go for two days, according to the note. It said she wanted time to think some things over. It didn't say what those things were."

Mullen said, "Are they sure it was from her?"

Anna said, "Her husband said it was her handwriting and that was confirmed. It didn't look like it was written under duress."

Cullen said, "The whole thing was out of character. The husband, James Bosko, denied any problems in the marriage. They'd celebrated their anniversary the day before she left. He'd taken the day off work. Anyway, she didn't return on Friday and he called the cops the next day."

The chief peered at them over wire-rimmed glasses. "They check him out?"

"They didn't find anything. He was putting in long days at the hospital—except for the day he took off before she disappeared—then was home with the kids at night. But that doesn't mean he couldn't have hired somebody to kill her. We plan to look at him very closely. It's not going to be easy, but if there's something there, we'll find it."

Anna said, "The older daughter called him on the Wednesday when she came home from school and found her mother gone."

Frowning, the chief considered this in silence. On the desk in front of her, crime scene photos showed skeletal remains in an excavated area of about a dozen square feet near the barn. The grave had been a couple feet deep, suggesting the killer had been in no hurry.

Anna said, "Fast forward a couple of decades and her remains turn up at a farm near New Hampshire." She explained how Lisa Bosko was identified through a DNA match with a daughter.

He said, "We just interviewed Nicole Bosko and I think she may be able to remember more about what happened."

The chief raised her eyebrows above the thin red frames of her glasses.

He said, "She remembered visiting the farm where her mother's body was found as a little kid. There are probably other things she can remember. It could be key."

"How old was she?"

"Five. It's quite possible there are more memories there."

The chief frowned. "What if she was lying about remembering going to the farm with her mother? Doesn't she have a record? She may not be trustworthy."

Anna said, "About ten years ago she and a boyfriend crashed a boat. I remember it. There was a lot of talk at the time. It was a minor scandal in Riverton, a big embarrassment for her father."

Mullen drummed a pen on the desk. "The father and sister are coming back when?"

He said, "In a couple of days. We've read over their transcripts from the time Lisa Bosko went missing, but there wasn't much there. I'm not sure we'll be able to get more out of them now, but we'll sure as hell try."

Anna said, "We know Nicole Bosko was interviewed, but the transcript of the interview was missing from what we got sent. We'll be getting another box in a day or two, so we hope it's in there. She must have made some reference to a man her mother talked to on the phone—this was just before she went missing—because the father and sister were asked about it but said they didn't know anything. We'll follow up with them as soon as we can reach them."

The chief took off her glasses, grabbed a tissue, and cleaned them. Finished, she set them on the desk. "What if there's nothing more to remember? Or what if she doesn't want to help find out who killed her mother? The last time she saw her was supposedly twenty years ago."

He and Anna exchanged a look. Anna said, "I think she wants to. She was pretty upset. She was pretty angry at her mother for leaving, but now that she knows her mother was murdered, she'll want to help." Anna gave him a quick look. They didn't want to tell Mullen that Nicole Bosko might be very reluctant to get involved.

Mullen was frowning again. "Back up for a sec. When was Lisa Bosko last seen?"

Anna said, "Wednesday morning. She saw the girls off to school in the morning. The older one was picked up earlier, because she had some event. The younger one was the last to see her mother. She told us today she remembers nothing of it, but she was probably interviewed, so we'll look at the transcript, see if we can jog her memory."

Cullen said, "The girls came home from school and apparently the mother wasn't there. Her car was in the driveway. They called the father and he came home and said he found the note in an envelope on his bedside table. It said she would be gone two days. The father called the cops on Saturday. The search started that afternoon and continued for five days, but they didn't find anything. There was a big search, because the husband had connections and put a lot of pressure on."

Anna said, "The house was in a forested area near a lake. The husband still lives there."

Mullen said, "Did they search the lake?"

He said, "Divers went in but they didn't find anything."

Anna said, "At the time, there was some talk she'd been having an affair but it was never confirmed."

Mullen perked up. "What if it was true? What if she was having an affair and the guy picked her up? Maybe she thought they were going away together but instead he killed her."

Cullen said, "If there was a guy, maybe Nicole knew him. She and her mother spent a lot of time together because she didn't start school until that fall. I'm sure if we question her some more she'll be able to remember something. She may even have met the guy."

Anna said, "Or maybe she knows something about the father. They're definitely not close."

He said, "We have to track down witnesses, see who's still around, and interview them again. Like Anna said, we haven't been able to reach the other daughter and the husband, but we'll keep trying."

The chief stood up. "I've got a meeting. Come up with something fast, okay? Something concrete to justify spending resources on this. You'll be pulled off it if and when you're needed elsewhere."

Cullen rubbed his temple. Already, she wanted to shove the case to the back burner. No doubt she'd ride their asses the whole way. "Somebody has to pay for killing this woman," he said, clenching his fists as frustration swept through him. "And there's always the chance the killer's still out there."

Never mind that whenever he saw Lisa Bosko's reconstruction she seemed to be speaking to him, telling him to find out who killed her. How do you explain that? Or how do you explain that he'd become a cop because of cases like this. That still haunting him was the face of a friend's sister who'd disappeared, never to be found, when he was a teenager.

Mullen held up her hand to stop further protest. "I know, I know. But the stats on cold cases make this a long shot. I'd rather spend my money on fresh cases. They have a way better chance of being solved. So find something. Fast."

CHAPTER FOUR

Outside the police station, the sun had gone into hiding again and the streets of Riverton were bleak and gray. Nicky had refused Cullen Fraser's offer of a drive, not wanting to spend another minute in his company, opting instead for a cab that dropped her off at her apartment building fifteen minutes later.

She trudged up to her third-floor apartment, went to the bathroom and washed up, then borrowed a cell phone from a woman she knew on the second floor to call the shelter. Michelle was already back. Nicky let out a huge sigh, then explained what had happened. She kept the details to a minimum and her boss gave her a week off, assured her Michelle would be well looked after and promised to have someone drop off her phone.

An hour later, when a coworker came by with the phone, Nicky accepted her condolences but didn't let her into the apartment. It wasn't polite, but they'd never been more than acquaintances and now wasn't the time to become BFFs.

She tried calling her sister, but got voice mail and left a message asking her to call. She took a bath, slipped into pajamas, and sat on the sofa. It was evening, already dark, but she lacked the energy to get up to turn on a light. She couldn't eat, couldn't do anything, it seemed, but cry. For all her efforts over the years to forget her mother, Lisa Bosko's face was in sharp focus now and memories came flooding back. Her mother singing her to sleep, hugging her father, digging in the garden. And taking photographs, always taking photographs. Now that she was letting herself remember, she couldn't turn the tap off.

In bed that night, Nicky tossed and turned. The lifeless eyes on the sculpture stared at her accusingly. A sleeping pill might have been a good idea, but she didn't have any and it seemed like a copout, anyway. At four in the morning, she got up and checked her phone. Nothing from Karina. Did she know? How would her father react? Remembering his stoicism in the years after her mother disappeared, her stomach twisted.

In the living room, she fired up her laptop computer and found a brief news item about the discovery of her mother's body. An excavator operator had found remains while digging on the property of an abandoned farmhouse in Lisette. The report struck her as brutally impersonal and she felt her throat go scratchy.

She closed the page, decided to see if there were any stories from twenty years ago, when her mother went missing. Ten minutes later, she found a photocopy of a short item from an old newspaper. But the story, headlined SEARCH ENDS FOR MISSING RIVERTON-AREA WOMAN, didn't tell her anything new. After five days, finding nothing and with no hint of foul play, police had called off the search. There was a headshot of her mother, cropped from a family photo, but no quotes from her father. How hard had they searched? It was impossible to tell from the story.

Fifteen minutes later, unable to find anything else, she shut the computer down. There were so many stories of missing people, many of them children, but adults too. Sometimes people were found alive, sometimes bodies were identified, but often there was nothing. Many other families were left waiting, never learning the truth about what had happened. She swallowed a lump in her throat.

She must have dozed because the next thing she knew it was morning and the sun was creeping across the parquet floor in her living room. At eight, she showered and got dressed, made coffee, then called her friend Emily Blackstock, who promised to come over as soon as she could, sometime before noon.

At nine, her cell phone rang. It was a strange area code and she considered not answering it, but then realized it could be Karina.

"Hi, Nicole." It was Karina.

Nicky sat down, felt tears well up. "Hi."

"You should have called."

"I'm sorry. I tried but just got voice mail." She sighed. Here she was, already apologizing for something she had no control over.

"We're catching a ride to Port-au-Prince tomorrow morning. We're at a hospital in Cap-Hatien now. There's an afternoon flight to New York."

"I'm glad you could make it out so quickly. Are you okay?"

There was a silence for a moment, and then her sister said, "It's such a shock. Her taking off was one thing—"

"We can't be sure she did take off."

"Of course she did. There was a note." Her tone was clipped, dismissive and it wasn't hard to picture the frown that usually went with it.

Nicky decided to let it go. What if someone had forged it, or her mother had been forced to write it? But that hardly sounded plausible. This was real life, not a movie. She said, "How is dad?"

"He's taking it pretty hard but he insisted on working this morning. There was a newborn having seizures. He had to help."

Nicky pulled in a deep breath. Oh yeah, that was her father. A strong believer in putting others first, and carrying on no matter what. In the years after his wife's disappearance, he hadn't complained, opting instead to shut himself away in his study for an hour or two. The flip side was his reluctance to talk about her at all. Except one time when Nicky had come home from school, crying, because some kids had teased her about her mother, saying she'd run off with another man. Her father had said to ignore them; her mother was an honorable woman. She hadn't understood the meaning of the word honorable but the fierceness in his tone had made his sentiment clear.

Karina said, "He wanted to talk to you, but I said we could meet up when we got home."

Nicky gritted her teeth. It wasn't a conscious decision on Karina's part, but why did she always have to be the buffer between her and her father? Did she expect her to say something to upset him?

Her sister sniffled. "I almost forgot. He wanted to make sure you didn't call Uncle Steve. He wanted to be the one to break it to him."

"Of course." Uncle Steve was her father's brother, his only sibling, three years younger.

They talked for a few more minutes, and then Karina said, "We'll take a cab from the airport. We'll be in late, but we should be able to meet up. Can you come to the house?" She didn't wait for an answer. "Don't do anything until we get there, all right?"

Nicky tensed. "What do you mean? What do you think I'm going to do?"

Karina said, "We have to stick together in this, that's all. We'll talk about it more when we get home. Just let me handle it from here on in."

She frowned. What was Karina talking about?

Her sister's tone softened. "Love you, Nicole. See you soon."

Karina hung up before Nicky could respond. Sitting down, she swallowed the sharp taste in her mouth. Already, Karina was taking over, being the big sister. Some things were never going to change. But maybe it wouldn't be such a bad thing. Nicky didn't have a great track record of handling things. And at least Karina had her father's best interests at heart. That was the main thing.

* * *

At her kitchen table that afternoon, Nicky watched her friend Emily Blackstock grate cheddar cheese onto a wooden cutting board. She said, "You don't have to do this."

Emily said, "Are you kidding? It's the least I could do. Have you eaten anything today?"

She shook her head. How could she survive without Emily, her one true friend? They were so alike in so many ways. Emily had dropped by an hour earlier and in that time Nicky had shed a river of tears, not bothering to try to stop the flow. She'd let Emily hug her, even though she didn't normally do hugs.

Emily said, "Have you spoken to your dad?"

"Not yet, but I talked to Karina for a few minutes this morning. They're coming home tomorrow. She advised me not to do anything until they come."

Emily pulled a face. "What does she think you're going to do?" Emily had a rocky relationship with her mother and knew all about messy family dynamics. They often commiserated.

"Heaven knows. Only Karina has the power to make me feel like a total boob for no reason at all." She took a sip of coffee. "I wouldn't be able to do anything even if I wanted. My mind is mush. The same thoughts keep running through my head. I keep thinking about my mother and how unfair it all is."

"You've never talked much about your mom."

"I got pretty good about putting her out of my mind. I still don't remember a lot. I was pretty young. But it's got to be awful for my dad and Karina. This is going to hit them so much harder. Especially my dad."

"Your dad will be okay, Nicky. Karina will make sure of it. It's you I'm worried about."

"I'll be okay." She stood up and walked to the kitchen window, which looked out onto a parking lot three stories below. She'd been in this apartment nearly two years, the longest she'd stayed in any place since she was sixteen. She'd been thinking of moving on. The apartment was dingy and too small to have people over and she could afford a better place. She sighed. That seemed such a silly thing to have worried about now.

Turning back, she watched her friend flip two grilled cheese sandwiches in a frying pan on top of the stove. "How's Matt?" Matt Herrington was her boyfriend.

Emily's dazzling green eyes lit up as she put the sandwiches on two small plates, then carried them to the table. "He's fine, busy, bugging me about setting a date."

Nicky sat down. "Usually it's the other way around."

Emily got two glasses of milk, then joined her. "We were going to have it in December, but then my mother said she was going to Europe in late November. Apparently Frank has never been to Europe and they plan to tour around for a couple of months. Now I'm thinking we should just elope." Frank was her mother's fiancé.

Nicky nodded, took a bite of her sandwich. "Maybe you should. You didn't want a big fuss anyway." She chuckled. "Maybe if you dyed your hair black again and chopped it off like when you were on the run last year your mother would encourage you to elope."

Emily laughed. "Now there's an idea." She narrowed her eyes. "I can see what you're doing, by the way."

Nicky, about to take a sip of milk, put the glass down. "What?"

"You're trying to deflect attention. This isn't about me. It's about you."

"We've talked about me nonstop." At her friend's look, she said, "I'm sorry. I'm not very good at discussing my feelings. I don't have to tell you that." Tears stinging her eyes, she said, "You haven't seen a picture of my mom, have you? Come on, I'll show you."

They put the dishes in the sink, then went to the living room and sat down. Nicky had pulled a shoebox containing family pictures out of the closer earlier, but hadn't built up the nerve to go through them yet. She hadn't looked at them in years, couldn't even remember how she'd ended up with them. Removing a big elastic band encircling the box, she opened the lid to reveal several hundred pictures jammed in haphazardly.

She riffled through the photos, found one of her mother and looked at it for a long moment before passing it to Emily. "There aren't many of my mother, but I have a few."

Emily's jaw dropped. "You look like her a lot. How old was she in this picture?"

"I'm not sure. She was barely thirty when she died." Fresh tears wet her eyes. "It's so awful, to think how some bastard stole her life. She was so young." She grabbed a tissue, wiped her eyes. "I don't know if I can forgive myself. I used to hate her, blame her for my problems."

Emily put a hand on her arm. "You can't blame yourself,

Nicky. You didn't have any idea what had happened. And you didn't have it easy."

"That doesn't excuse it. And maybe I didn't have it easy, but I did it to myself, didn't I? It's like my whole life has been a lie. I blamed everything on her. I mean, what kind of mother just abandons her family? I hated her for not even bothering to call, just to say hello. Now I know why."

Emily hugged her, then drew back and looked her in the eye. "Don't blame yourself. You had no idea. And it sounds like everybody just assumed she had taken off. Didn't you tell me your father gave you the idea she might have left because of you?"

"Somehow I always felt that, but I'm thinking now maybe he didn't. I was pretty messed up for quite a few years. Maybe I just talked myself into believing she'd left because I was such a handful."

"But she left a note, didn't she? I remember you saying something about that."

"I don't know what it said. There were rumors she'd had an affair. But nothing was ever proven." She rubbed her temples. "I'll have to ask my dad about it, see what he says. But I don't think he believed those rumors."

Nicky grabbed a handful of pictures and began sorting through them.

Emily said, "Do the police have any leads?"

"If they do, they're not telling me. We didn't exactly get off on the right foot."

Emily sighed. "Well, you did right to protect the runaway, not many would have done what you did. But you got yourself into a whole lot of hassle because of it."

Nodding, she bit her lip. "That's for sure. I don't think I made a good impression on the cops. Actually, I know I made quite a bad one."

Emily raised her eyebrows. "You're not exactly known for your love of the cops, Nicky."

"You've got a point there. Now they seem to think I may be able to remember things that will help them."

"Do you?"

"Of course not. I hardly remember anything. But try explaining it to them. They called a couple of times this morning, but I let them go to voice mail. I can't handle them right now."

"Did you listen to the messages? Maybe they have new information."

"I doubt it, but I'll check later. I am starting to remember a few more things, but nothing important."

"Like what?"

"Just little things. Like my mother seeing me off to school. And in the afternoon, when I got off the bus, she'd be waiting." Tears rolled down her cheeks. "From what I do remember of her, it's obvious she was a great mom. I can see that now."

An hour later, they'd been through every photograph in the box. Most of the pictures had been taken after her mother disappeared and they found only three of her mother. She picked up a picture of her, Karina, and their father. They were on a beach somewhere, obviously on vacation although she couldn't remember when it was or where. Nicky was in the foreground, crouched down to examine something in the sand, while her father and Karina held hands in the background. Her father was slimmer then, his hair darker.

Emily looked at it. "Did your mother take this?"

She nodded. "I'm pretty sure. I think I remember us going somewhere on a trip. I'll have to ask Dad about it."

"You look a bit like your father, too, the shape of your face, your eyes. But Karina really looks like him."

She smiled. "I used to think I was adopted. I was such a square peg in a round hole. I'm talking about after my mom left." She paused a beat. "It's pretty obvious now that I wasn't."

After Emily left, Nicky, feeling restless, decided to pop into the small grocery store down the street for some fruit. She ran a comb through her hair and grabbed her shoulder bag.

At the store, she ended up picking up a couple of things, more than she needed: crackers, fruit, frozen yogurt. She got in one of the lines to pay, picking the cashier with the purple hair, a young girl who was superfast. She never said much, either, which suited Nicky just fine.

Exiting the store, she put her bag down, fished in her shoulder bag for her sunglasses, and popped them on. Standing up, she pivoted on the sidewalk in the direction of her apartment.

Cullen Fraser stood in front of her, blocking her way.

CHAPTER FIVE

Cullen Fraser put his hand up and stepped back to avoid a collision with Nicole Bosko.

He couldn't see her eyes behind those sunglasses, which was probably a good thing, since it wasn't hard to imagine them shooting daggers at him.

She slung her bag over her shoulder. "Do you make a habit of banging into people? Or is it just me?"

"Actually, it's just you," he said evenly. "You have a way of not looking where you're going."

A buff guy in board shorts jogging by glanced back to check her out. She was wearing a green army jacket and faded jeans, and she had her hair twisted into a messy knot at the back of her head, but it wasn't hard to see why he'd wanted a second look at her lovely face and long, lean body.

She shifted the grocery bag she was carrying into her other hand. "Well, now that we've got that settled, do you mind moving out of my way?"

Clearing his throat, he reminded himself to keep his cool. "I have to ask you some questions."

"I've already told you everything I know."

He took a breath. "I was hoping you were able to remember more about what happened when your mother went missing. Can I walk you home?" She looked away, huffed, then nodded. He reached out a hand. "Can I carry your groceries?" She thought about it for a second, then shoved the bag at him.

A car drove by, a heavy bass beat thumping. When the noise had died down, he said, "Do you remember anything more about the last day you saw your mother?"

She shot him a look. "No."

He ground his teeth. For the life of him, he couldn't understand why she didn't want to at least try to help him. "Have you even tried?"

She stopped, wheeled on him. "Of course I've tried. I've thought about nothing but that."

He held a hand up, aware he'd gone too far. But she was pushing his buttons again. Her dislike of him, and the simmering resentment against cops that came off her like a bad smell, brought out the worst in him.

He said, "I'm sorry."

She wasn't to be placated. "Do you think I don't care what happened to my mother?"

Her voice had risen, and an elderly man walking toward them glared at him. Bosko started walking again and Cullen followed, shaking his head.

"I don't remember anything specific about that day. You'll have to take my word for that."

"Had your father left for work?"

"Probably. I started going to school that fall and I remember when I got up, he was usually gone." Her tone was clipped and she spoke without looking at him.

"What about your sister? Where was she?"

"Karina had already eaten. She was getting a ride to school so she could be there early. It was probably to do with some school group she was involved in. I remember she didn't take the bus."

He nodded encouragingly. "Anything else?"

"My mom was wearing a dress." She shot him a glance. "Don't ask me how I remember, but I do. And she had a lunch packed for me." She stopped, stared ahead. "She said good-bye to me outside the front door. She kissed me. The school bus picked me up just down the street and she waved at me when I was on the bus."

"Did she seem happy? Sad?"

She shrugged. "I don't remember. Normal, I think."

They reached her apartment building. She turned to him. "Any more questions?"

"I'm afraid so."

She got out her key, opened the door, and led him up a set of stairs to the third floor. Another key opened the door to her apartment at the end of the hallway. Following her in, he slipped off his shoes, walked behind her to the kitchen, and put the shopping bag on the counter.

She disappeared into the bathroom. The apartment had a small galley kitchen and a living room with just enough room for the love seat and chair, old and mismatched, stuffed into it.

A small half-moon dining table was squeezed against a wall off the kitchen.

Marlee's place couldn't be more different. It was a new loft downtown, bright and open, bought with help from her parents. This place was a quarter the size but it was somehow cozy, with colorful pillows and books everywhere.

Thinking of his ex-girlfriend, he gritted his teeth. She'd texted him that morning, saying she was available if he wanted to talk. He hadn't replied. What was there to talk about? They'd been going out for three years, had even talked about getting married, settling down. Then two days ago she'd told him she was leaving him for another cop. Now he was left wondering for how long she'd been seeing the other cop behind his back.

Nicole walked into the kitchen and started emptying the shopping bag, putting yogurt and vegetables in her refrigerator and apples in a yellow enamel bowl on the counter.

Finished, she turned to him. "What else did you want to ask?" Her eyes were puffy and red.

Sitting down at the table, he took out a notepad and pen. "What happened after you got home from school?"

"I don't remember clearly. Karina and I came home together off the bus. Mom wasn't there. Karina went looking for her." She leaned against the counter, twirled a long strand of dark, silky hair around her finger. Her anger seemed to have dissipated, as if she didn't have the energy to maintain it. For now, anyway.

His mind went quiet for a moment as he drank in her face with its strong, carved features, then her body, slim and boyish except for those firm, round breasts that molded to the fabric of her shirt. It was the body of a dancer, lithe and graceful.

His pulse quickening, he looked away again, pretended to jot down some notes. It was humiliating. He didn't even like her and she sure as hell didn't like him.

She had said something and now looked at him expectantly.

He said, "I'm sorry. What were you saying?"

Her brown eyes probed. "You asked what happened after we came home from school that day. I said it was unusual but we weren't too worried." At his nod, she continued. "Karina said Mom must have gone out, but she'd be back. But she didn't come back."

Her eyes glistening, she walked to the kitchen window above the sink, looked out. After a moment, she wiped her eyes with her hands, then turned back to him. "Would you like a coffee? Water?"

"No thanks."

She walked into the living room and sat down on the sofa. He pivoted in his seat so he was facing her. "What happened next? After your mother didn't return?"

"My sister called my father."

"How much time did she wait?"

The tears started again, and her eyes seemed even larger because they were wet. She blinked, looked away. "It might have been a half hour or an hour, but that's a guess."

"Are you okay?"

"I'm fine." Her reply was curt. "Please continue."

Aware of a tightness in his chest, he stared at her a moment, then glanced at his notes. "How long before your father came home?"

"I don't remember."

"Did you eat? Watch TV?"

"My sister made me a peanut butter sandwich. She gave me a glass of milk, too. We weren't allowed to watch TV before supper." She sighed. "You should talk to my sister about this. She was a lot older. She'll be a lot more help than I am."

He ignored that. "Did your parents ever argue?"

She shot him a disapproving glare. "Not that I can remember."

"Not even about you?"

Her brows narrowed. "They had trouble with me, but I don't remember them arguing about me."

"What sort of trouble?"

She shrugged. "You asked me about this yesterday. I'm not sure. After my mother was gone, my father took me to a psychiatrist. I took medication for attention deficit for a few years."

"Do you mind if I ask if you take it now?"

"Of course I mind." She crossed her arms, hesitated a moment before she said, "The answer is no. I haven't for years. I guess I grew out of it." She spoke evenly, but a faint bitterness in her tone hinted at more complex feelings underneath.

"Do you remember telling the police your mother had a male friend she spoke with on the phone?"

She bristled. "Not at all. I would have said so if I'd remembered and I don't even remember being interviewed. Where did that information come from?"

"I received a one-page fax today, a summary of an interview police conducted with you six days after your mother's disappearance. They talked to you for a few minutes in the presence of a social worker."

She sat forward, her spine stiff. "And?"

"You told police your mother spoke twice on the phone to a man who was not your father. You claimed it was the same man both times and your mother seemed upset. You said she cried after one of the calls."

She blanched, shook her head slowly from side to side. "I don't remember."

"The phone calls or what you told police?"

"Neither." She wrung her hands. "Maybe I made it up."

"The cop who conducted the interview, Constable Melanie Wright, didn't think so."

She stood up, looked out the living room window. "It doesn't make sense. Karina or my father would have heard the calls, too."

"Unless she waited until they weren't around. Maybe your mother underestimated your powers of observation because you were so young. She thought it was safe to talk in your presence."

He braced for her anger, but when she turned around, there was no sign of it. Instead, the look of vulnerability in her face made him catch his breath. With her guard down, it wasn't hard to imagine her as a young, frightened child.

She said, "What else did I say?"

"The summary seems to focus on this one part of the interview. I'm still waiting for the full transcript. I should get it in a day or so."

She nodded, and the vulnerable look was gone. Her eyes were steady, her jaw set. "Can that be it for now? My dad and sister will be home coming home from Haiti tomorrow. You'll be able to ask them about this. I'm sure you'll get better answers."

* * *

Nicky didn't see her father and sister until two days later. Their flight from Haiti had been delayed the previous evening, and they'd been too exhausted for a visit that night. On Thursday evening, Nicky drove thirty minutes to her father's house, a two-story Cape Cod her parents had built in the early years of their marriage in the tiny community of Stephenville. It was a private spot, set in the woods above a lake, and the only family home she'd ever lived in, although for all its familiarity she had a difficult time summoning feelings of warmth about it. The house somehow felt less like home than a symbol of a past she'd rather forget.

Her father opened the door as she walked up the front step. There were dark shadows under his eyes and his pallor was ashen. It was as if he'd aged ten years in the month since she'd run into him in a coffee shop in Riverton.

She swallowed hard as he drew her to him and enveloped her in a hug. Surprised, she hugged him back. They both had a natural aversion to such gestures.

"How are you?" She met his red-rimmed eyes with an ache in her throat. "Are you okay, Dad?"

"There have been people coming and going all day." He voice was low and he spoke slowly. A big, strong man, her father's shoulders now drooped and his body was curved inward, as if it had shrunk. "It's exhausting. And of course Haiti wasn't exactly a vacation."

She should have come earlier. There was no excuse, other than feeling worse than the day before. It was as if she were in a fog, adrift, disconnected from everything and everybody. It had been an effort to get in the car and drive here.

In the foyer, Karina and Uncle Steve were talking to a middle-aged woman who was slipping into a pair of flats. Nicky didn't recognize her, but the woman shook her hand and offered condolences. She kissed James Bosko before leaving.

Off the hallway, in the formal living room, the lid was up on Karina's piano, a high-gloss ebony baby grand. She must have been playing it today. As a teenager, Karina had spent endless hours sitting at it, practicing some Schubert sonata over and over again.

Nicky hugged her sister and uncle, who were both red-eyed, then followed her father to the great room at the back of the house, made a few years back when the wall between the family room and kitchen had been knocked down. He sat down on the sofa and she chose a wing chair by the window looking out over the rocky shoreline of the lake. Karina set a glass of wine on the table beside Nicky, then sat beside their father.

After several minutes of small talk, there was a pause and her father turned to her. "I hope the police didn't bother you too much."

She shook her head. "There wasn't anything I could tell them. Have they talked to you?" She glanced at her father, then Karina.

Karina said, "They came here this morning and interviewed both of us, separately." Her voice was harsh, her face tense and eyes puffy. She'd inherited their father's wide face and strong nose, which made her look stern.

Their father leaned back on the sofa. "It's okay, Karina. We must do everything we can to help them."

Karina said, "But that's the thing. I'm not sure how much we can help them. And it'll probably mean they'll drag Mom's name through the mud again. And our family with it."

Her uncle flushed pink. "Surely not."

Her father said, "We have to be prepared for everything. And that may be an unintended consequence."

Watching them, Nicky wanted to point out the danger of a renewal of gossip about the family wasn't as important as finding out who had killed Lisa Bosko but she held her tongue. Her father, well known in the Riverton area, would suffer that consequence more.

He clutched his chest. "But we have each other, and that's the most important thing. I know it's a cliché, but it's true."

Her face flushed, Karina seemed about to break into tears. "They should have done more when Mom first went missing." She took a sip of wine and looked at her father, waiting for his response, maybe even his approval.

Her father frowned. "I can't disagree with you there."

Nicky's breath hitched. She leaned forward. "I thought they did a thorough search."

Karina exchanged a glance with her father. "You were a bit young to remember properly." A hint of acid tinged her tone. Karina had a disapproving way of speaking to Nicky that she didn't always try to hide.

Ignoring her, Nicky addressed her father. "Was the search not thorough?"

James Bosko rubbed his temples. "I always felt they weren't

serious about trying to find her. I remember one of cops at the time saying she probably left of her own free will."

She swallowed. "Why did they think that? Was it because of the note?"

Her father looked at her sympathetically. "They told you about that? I hope you didn't get the wrong idea. She just needed a couple of days."

It seemed likely there was more to it, but she held her tongue again, not wanting to upset her father. She would seek more details later.

Karina poured herself another glass of wine, but Nicky declined, saying she had to drive. Karina would stay overnight in the apartment above the garage, but the offer wasn't made to Nicky because they knew she wouldn't accept it. She hadn't slept in this house in half a dozen years.

Her father took a sip of whiskey from the tumbler in his hand, met her eye. "Like I said, we should do everything we can to help the police."

Her sister said, "Do you think there's any hope they'll find out who did this, after this many years?"

Her father sighed heavily. "Their chances will be higher if we help them."

The conversation died down and after a moment her uncle, who had barely spoken a word, said, "Do you have time off work, Nicole?"

"They gave me a week and said I could take longer if I needed it. I'll make my mind up later."

He said, "It's a big shock. You may need more time."

She smiled at him, struck again by how much he and her father looked alike. They had the same dark eyes, the same kind face, and they were the same height, although her uncle was slimmer, with a wiry physique that suggested he got a lot of exercise. Three years younger than James, he was an engineer who owned a company that made gas station canopies. He'd divorced a dozen years ago after seven or eight years of marriage. Like her father, he had never remarried, although not for lack of opportunity.

Karina said, "They're not expecting me back at the hospital for another week, so I'm taking time, too. I'll stay with Daddy."

Her father said, "I told you it wasn't necessary."

"Of course it is."

Her father rolled his eyes, but there was a smile on his face. Nicky felt a prick of jealousy. Karina was the obedient daughter, whereas Nicky had constantly rebelled, stopping only when she'd finally realized she was hurting herself just as much as her father. Was this a chance for her to make amends?

Karina was looking at her. "Do you remember that day?"

"I'm sorry, what day?"

Karina smiled. "The day you got angry at Mom? She wanted you to wear a dress. We were having a family photo taken." A false brightness in her voice suggested she was trying to lighten the mood, to make sure they remembered the good times.

She nodded. "I remember. It was taken in this room." Her mother and father had sat side by side on the sofa and she'd sat on her mother's lap, while Karina stood beside her father. "I was wearing a white blouse with frills down the front and a skirt."

"Mom was so upset," Karina said.

"I don't remember that at all." In her recollection, her mother had laughed off her refusal to wear a dress. How odd that they had such conflicting memories of the same event.

Karina laughed. "It doesn't matter. But it's nice to think of those days, how happy we were."

Her father smiled, perhaps aware of Karina's motive, but not minding. It was the first time they'd talked about her mother in years, and it seemed strange she had to have died to become a topic of conversation. It was as if they were role-playing to find a comfortable way to act as a family, now that the subject of Lisa Bosko was no longer taboo.

Uncle Steve said, "Nicole, before you came, we were talking about holding a memorial service for your mother."

She smiled at her uncle, who'd always struck her as a quieter, softer version of her father. "Sounds like a good idea."

Karina said, "We thought maybe Daddy would give a eulogy, and maybe I would play something on the piano."

Her father said, "We want to make sure we honor your mother."

She nodded in agreement, wondering at the emotions he must be feeling. For many years her father had endured rumors about how his wife had abandoned her family. To find out, years later, that she hadn't must be a vindication of sorts. A new thought popped into her head, and suddenly her heart felt too big for her chest. Was it possible her father had not remarried because he had waited all those years for his wife to come back?

He said, "I'm not sure I'll be up to speaking, but I imagine Steve will step in if I can't."

Her uncle cleared his throat. "Uh, I'm not sure I can do that." His hesitancy was no surprise. It was common knowledge that Steve Bosko didn't like speaking in public. Refused to do it, in fact. Her father often told the story of how her uncle, at his brother's wedding, hadn't been able to deliver the opening speech at the reception.

Her father was having none of it. "For God's sake, Steve. I don't ask for much."

Steve Bosko's face flushed. He hesitated, then stammered, "Of course."

Nicky's stomach knotted. She would have happily stepped in and she wondered why her father hadn't asked. As to her uncle's response, she didn't know whether to feel admiration he'd agreed or irritation at her father for pushing him. In some ways, her uncle's relationship with his big brother mirrored her own with Karina, although there was a key difference: Karina's hold over her younger sibling was much more tenuous.

* * *

That night, back at home, Nicky opened the box of family photos again and dug around for a copy of the family portrait her sister had talked about. It was near the bottom of the box, a five-by-seven-inch photo, crinkled and yellowed with age. It was much as she remembered it. They all looked happy, including her mother, her nose crinkling as she smiled. No sign of anger.

She sat back. Her memories of those early years were dim, as if filtered through a dark, flimsy curtain. Had her family been happy? Karina seemed to be forging ahead with the idea they had been, and maybe she was right. What harm could it do? It seemed better than trying to dredge up memories that might only bring heartache.

Outside, darkness had descended like a curtain. She propped the photo against a lamp on the table beside the sofa, then went to the kitchen and made hot chocolate. She took a sip, but it was too hot and scalded the roof of her mouth.

In the living room, she turned on the table lamp and sat down. Try as she might, she couldn't stop thinking about her mother's last moments. Had she gone to the farm to take pictures and met up with a stranger, a stranger who had killed her? Or had she gone to the farm with somebody she knew? That seemed more likely. Had she tried to defend herself? Had she even had a chance?

Maybe some of those questions would never be answered. But the more she thought about it, the more she knew she had to find the answers. Otherwise, that gaping hollowness in her chest would never go away.

Her cell phone rang. She checked the number. Cullen Fraser. She hesitated a moment, then answered. "Hello."

He said hello, then cleared his throat. "There are two things I wanted to talk to you about."

His voice, deep and resonant, reminded her of guys who talked on the radio. But it seemed to have a catch, as if he had bad news.

"Okay."

"We are going to be issuing a press release tomorrow identifying your mother as a murder victim. I wanted to warn you."

She closed her eyes. "Have my father and sister been told?"

"We'll make sure they are informed."

Thinking of her father, she bit her lip to keep from crying. "And the other thing?"

"I have a copy of the transcript of your interview."

"And?"

"And I'd like to see you again." He cleared his throat. "Sorry, I didn't mean it to come out that way."

She rolled her eyes. "Don't worry. I have no fear you're going soft on me, detective."

From him, silence for a moment, then he said, "Can I come by? Tomorrow?" His voice was gruff.

Remembering what her father had said about helping the police, she swallowed the protest on her lips. Presumably there was something in the transcript to merit another interview. He certainly wasn't doing it for the fun of it.

He said, "Is eleven o'clock okay?"

"Fine." About to hang up, she hesitated. "Wait. I'll come to your office."

Nausea inducing as it was, the prospect of returning to the police station was the lesser of two evils. Cullen Fraser was too big a guy for her small apartment and she felt strangely uncomfortable being alone with him there. She didn't want him finding out anything more about her than was absolutely necessary, even if it was what books she read and the fat content of the yogurt she had for breakfast.

CHAPTER SIX

Cullen drummed his fingers on his desk and waited for Nicole Bosko to finish reading the transcript of the old interview. It was Friday morning and she'd shown up at the front desk downstairs at eleven o'clock sharp, not a minute sooner. She wore a cream-colored blouse and khaki pants and had her hair tied back in a ponytail, which emphasized her big eyes and high cheekbones.

Flipping to the second page, she glanced up for a moment, her face flushed. It occurred to him he'd never seen her smile and likely never would.

He rubbed the back of his neck. What the heck did it matter what she looked like if she smiled? He didn't even like her. Although he had to admit he disliked her a little less now than when they'd first met.

Glancing through the transcript again, he hoped it would jog her memory. The interview had taken place in the presence of Nola Bosko, her uncle's wife. Her father had apparently been out searching for the mother.

If he didn't come up with something soon, the chief was going to pull the plug on this case. He'd lost Anna that morning to a suspected murder-suicide in Riverton's north end.

Cullen thought about the father and sister. He'd interviewed them each twice. The sister hadn't said anything new, but James Bosko had claimed his wife had had a brief affair about two years before she disappeared. He was sure it had been long over by the time she disappeared and claimed his marriage had been stronger than ever. When he relayed this information to Nicole, she had looked surprised but said nothing.

Was James Bosko telling the truth? Hard to say, but the father had an alibi that had been checked thoroughly; there was no way Bosko could have left the hospital that day without a dozen people knowing about it. And there was no evidence he'd hired a hitman. Riverton was small enough it seemed likely that people would have known. Would have talked about it. His financial records had been examined at the time, but no large withdrawals had been made. He and Anna had been digging for a couple of days and had come up empty. There had been no insurance policy on Lisa Bosko, so nobody had benefited financially from her death. They'd also vetted Steve Bosko and found no sign he'd helped his brother cover any tracks. The younger brother had an alibi, too; he and his wife had been in Connecticut at a construction convention.

Now more than ever it seemed his best lead was Nicole

Bosko and what she could remember from two decades ago, especially given what she'd told the cops at the time. His eyes scanned for a section from the last page.

Const. Wright: Nicole, do you know what it means to tell the truth?

Nicole: It means not lying.

Const. Wright: Are you telling the truth when you say your mother talked to a man on the telephone?

Nicole: *Nods.*

Const. Wright: Who was the man?

Nicole: *Shrugs.*

Const. Wright: How do you know it was a man?

Nicole: You asked before.

Const. Wright: I'm asking you some things so we can be sure, so you won't have to keep coming back here. Okay?

Nicole: *Nods.*

Const. Wright: Are you sure it was a man on the phone?

Nicole: He had a man voice.

Const. Wright: Was it your daddy?

Nicole: *Shakes head no.*

Const. Wright: Why do you say it wasn't your daddy?

Nicole: *Shrugs.*

Const. Wright: Was it your daddy's voice?

Nicole: *Shakes head no.*

Const. Wright: Okay. What did your mom and this man on the telephone talk about?

Nicole: *Shrugs.*

Const. Wright: Okay, tell me—

Nicole: Mommy cried.

Const. Wright: Your mother cried? During the phone call?

Nicole: *Shrugs.*

Const. Wright: Was your mother crying when she was talking to the man?

Nicole: Mommy's scared.

Const. Wright: Who is she scared of? The man?

Nicole: Nods. Mommy's going away.

Const. Wright: She's going away? Where?

Nicole: I don't want to go.

Const. Wright: Did she want you to go with her?

Nicole: It's a secret.

Const. Wright: Did she ask you to keep it a secret?

Nicole : *Nods.*

Const. Wright : Well, you can tell me, because I'm with the police, okay?

Nicole : *Nods.*

Const. Wright : Were you going away with your mom?

Nicole: Nods.

Const. Wright : Were Karina and your daddy going?

Nicole: No.

Const. Wright: Just you and your mom?

Nicole: Nods. I'm scared. I want my daddy.

Note: Nicole started crying, wouldn't stop. Interview concluded 1:13 p.m.

Finished reading, Bosko stared at the transcript with an unfocused gaze.

He pinched his lips together. "Does the transcript trigger any memories?"

She put the transcript on the desk, then rubbed her face in her hands. "I'm not sure. Vaguely. Maybe."

"Vaguely? Like what?"

She looked up, her eyes narrowed. "Don't start on me again. I'm trying my best." Closing her eyes, she took a breath, opened them again. "Being in the police station is starting to come back. And being with my mom at home. My mom crying. I remember my mom crying."

He ran a hand through his hair. "What was she crying about?"

When Bosko looked up, her eyes were wet with tears. "I think she was upset, maybe scared."

"Okay."

Suddenly, she stiffened and her eyes widened.

He said, "What is it?"

"She wasn't just scared for herself. She was upset about something to do with me, too."

"You?"

"I remember her talking about us going away, the two of us." She wrapped a strand of hair around her finger and began twisting it. "I didn't want to. I'd just started school and hadn't come to dislike it yet. But she said I had to."

"You didn't tell anybody?"

"She said not to." She'd stopped crying but her voice croaked. "But it doesn't make sense. Why would she be worried about somebody trying to hurt us and not my dad or Karina?"

He considered this. "Depends on the motive. When was she was planning to go?"

She sat back, thinking. "I think it was soon. But I can't say for sure."

He said, "Maybe it had nothing to do with this supposed affair. Is it possible you could have seen something, maybe witnessed something illegal?"

She shook her head slowly. "I don't remember anything like that. And if I had, presumably I'd be dead, too, if that was the motive for killing her."

"Maybe we're approaching this all wrong. Maybe the man on the phone wasn't the same guy she'd been involved with. Maybe this was another man, somebody your mother feared, for whatever reason."

"Wouldn't she have told my father?"

He nodded. "You're right. Do you remember anything more about the man on the phone? What they talked about?"

She shook her head to indicate no.

He said, "Could he have been threatening your mother?"

"I just told you I don't remember. Maybe I'm wrong about her being scared." The words came out through clenched teeth.

"All right." Massaging his temples with his fingers, he tried to think. This was going nowhere fast.

Her eyes were wet and avoided his. "I'm sorry. I would give anything to remember, but I just can't."

He said, "Melanie Wright, the cop who interviewed you, quit the force four years later but I managed to track her down. She's selling real estate. I'm hoping to talk to her later in the day, see if she can remember anything else."

"Wouldn't she have put everything in her report?"

"It's worth a try."

A fat tear rolled down her cheek and she brushed it away with the back of her hand. "I do appreciate everything you're doing. I just wish I wasn't so useless."

His heart squeezed. "It's not your fault."

She blinked back tears. "What if I did make it all up? It's possible, you know. I'm so mixed up I don't know what's real and what's imagined. I think my sister and father's recollections are much more reliable."

Cullen thought about the father and sister. In their interviews with him and Anna, both had sworn they hadn't overheard any calls. James Bosko suggested it was possible Nicole had made up the calls to get attention. But what if she hadn't made them up? What if the affair hadn't been over and the father knew but wanted to cover it up to avoid rumors? He wouldn't have known his wife had been murdered, possibly by this man. Or maybe it had been over, but there had been threatening phones calls that his wife hadn't told him about.

Nicole scrubbed her face with her palms. "I think I've told you I had attention deficit disorder as a child. Apparently, having problems with communication—lying—can be part of that."

He said, "I don't—"

"Let me finish." She stared down at her hands. "I've messed up a lot of things. I caused my father and sister a lot of grief over the years. I got in trouble in school so many times my father's phone number was on speed dial at the principal's office."

"You're telling me this because?"

"Because you seem to be putting a lot of weight on what I said when I was five years old. I think that's a big mistake."

His breath caught at her vulnerable expression. She was waiting with those dark eyes for him to say something, maybe confirm the idea she was a worthless witness.

"I don't think it's a mistake. I don't think the fear and concern in that transcript is a lie. You may have had ADHD or whatever, but that doesn't make you a liar or a bad kid. And right now, that five-year-old kid is my best hope for solving this murder."

She looked at him, even more vulnerable.

Maybe it was the vulnerability. Or a lot of other things put together—her looks, intelligence, mettle. Whatever it was, something shifted in his heart and it began to pound a little faster.

Shit.

If he were to make a list of the least suitable women for him in Riverton, Nicole Bosko would top the list. Nobody else would come close.

He stood up. "Want some coffee?"

"No thanks."

He went to the kitchen, got a mug, and poured himself a cup of coffee. It was so wrong on so many counts, including the fact he'd just broken up with Marlee. He closed his eyes, massaged his neck to work out a kink.

Back in the office, he said, "There's something else. I spoke with one of your mother's friends yesterday. She confirms your mother had an affair."

"But we knew about the affair. You just told me my father confirmed it."

"Let me finish. She also said something to do with you had your mother worried."

* * *

Nicky said, "Really? What else did she say?" For a minute, he didn't say anything, just waited, watching her with those eyes. They looked a curious denim color in this light. If she didn't look away right now, she'd be hypnotized.

Somewhere along the line he'd rolled up his shirt sleeves. Veins popped on his ripped arms and the room seemed way too small for that much manliness. She could practically smell the testosterone.

He said, "She didn't recall very much, unfortunately, but she was left with the impression that your mother was scared that harm was going to come to you. But your mother wouldn't tell her why. She said she was going to handle it. That's why your memories are key. Your father and sister say they were unaware of these calls."

"You think they're lying?"

He shrugged. "It's possible one or both of them are. I intend to find out."

Why would her father lie? It didn't make sense. Everybody knew a murdered woman's husband was an easy suspect, but she didn't believe for a moment he was capable of murder. She said, "My father had nothing to do with my mother's death."

"How do you know?"

"Because I know him." Even to her own ears, it sounded feeble. But it was true. "And he wouldn't have hurt me. If he had, why kill my mother and not me? It doesn't make sense."

"Maybe you knew who the man she was having the affair with was."

"But I didn't. I'm sure of that. And I don't know now."

"Maybe you do. You said yourself it was a long time ago. Maybe you did but you have forgotten."

"I don't think so." She shook her head. "Who is this friend? The woman you talked to who knew my mother?"

He flipped the pages on a notepad. "Isabel McMahon."

A heavy feeling settled in her gut. Part of her had been hoping the woman had been some attention seeker who could be easily discounted. "I remember her. She lived down the road."

He said, "Your sister confirmed she was a good friend of your mother's. She said this woman would babysit the two of you sometimes."

She nodded. An image came to mind of a short, plump woman with blond hair worn twisted around her head in a bun. "I haven't thought of her in years. I think she was Norwegian."

"That explains the accent. It's still quite strong." He cleared his throat. "Your mother didn't tell her the man's name or any details, but she did tell her she'd had an affair."

"Had?"

"It had apparently been over for a couple of years when they talked about it, at least according to what your mother told her. She said your mother felt guilty."

This only made things more confusing. "And my mother told her she was scared?"

He flipped through the notepad again. "She said your mother only referred to it in passing one time, when they had gone out for a walk. It was something to do with you."

"When did this happen?"

"About a month before she disappeared."

Her mouth soured. "That's a whole lot of nothing."

"No, unfortunately, your mother didn't tell her more, but it does confirm that your mother was worried about something."

Suddenly tired again, she rubbed her eyes. Last night had been another night with little sleep. Perhaps she should see her doctor. "Was Mrs. McMahon sure the relationship between my mother and this man was over?"

"Definitely, according to what your mother told her. Your mother had apparently loved this man, might still have, but she wasn't going to leave your father."

"Maybe this man was angry because she wouldn't leave my father." She thought about it some more. "Or maybe mom changed her mind and didn't tell Mrs. McMahon. If—and that's a big if—if my recollection is accurate, she was going to go away."

"And take you with her."

But instead of taking her away, the man had killed her. It was possible. The thought that somebody whom her mother had loved had also murdered her sent a chill through her.

She shook her head suddenly. "Wait a minute. Did Mrs. McMahon tell the police about the affair at the time?"

He shook his head no. "When she heard about the note, she

thought your mother had run away with this man."

"But my mother told her she wasn't going to."

"She now regrets not telling police. She just assumed your mother was alive."

If Mrs. McMahon had gone to the police, and if the police had believed Nicky, would it have all turned out differently? She wrung her hands. It was useless to speculate on that now.

She said, "Have you spoken to my father about this?" When he nodded, she said, "What happens now?"

"We have quite a few people we still have to interview. People who were around at the time she went missing. And we've had a few calls this morning, after we identified your mother as the murder victim."

"What if they're just crank calls?"

"Some of them might be, but there will be useful leads, too."

It was best not to read too much into his hopeful tone. She said, "Has the investigation at the farm wrapped up?"

He nodded. "Why do you ask?"

"I was just curious," she said, not wanting to explain the need for her to visit the place where her mother was last alive. She'd just wanted to make sure the police weren't still there.

CHAPTER SEVEN

Five days later, Lisa Bosko's memorial service was held at a funeral home in downtown Riverton. The chapel, a long and dimly lit room with a peaked ceiling and seating for one hundred people, was already half full when Nicky arrived with Emily and Matt.

As they walked to the front up the carpeted aisle, an ex-boyfriend sitting at the end of the row nearest the aisle turned and nodded at Nicky. She returned the nod, surprised Jason Spidell had come. A girl who looked barely out of high school leaned against him, staring down at a cell phone in her lap. On the other side of the girl was Jason's father, Allan, who had once employed Nicky's mother as a part-time bookkeeper.

She sat at the front next to her sister, while Emily and Matt found seats several rows back. Her father, sitting on the other side of Karina, offered a grim smile, then stared at an oversized framed photograph of his wife on the altar. Her mother's remains had not been released, and there was no casket. On the other side of her father sat his brother, Steve. The murmur of voices all but drowned out the faint organ music piped in through speakers.

She turned to Karina, who was dressed in a crispy navy blue suit. Her cheeks were pale and her eyes red. "Are you all right?"

Karina leaned in to whisper. "It's an awful thing to say, but I'll be glad when this is over. The phone never stops ringing. We don't get a moment's peace."

Nicky smoothed her skirt, then tugged at the sleeve of her blouse. It wasn't hard to imagine. Her father and sister had a wide circle of friends and acquaintances. Nicky lived mostly under the radar, her cell phone number a closely guarded secret.

Karina said, "Are you okay? Will you come to the house after?"

Nicky squeezed her sister's hand. "Of course I'll come." She wanted to tell Karina not to worry about her, but worrying was in Karina's DNA. After their mother disappeared, Karina had been forced into a hybrid mother-sister role she hadn't yet shed. How she must have longed for their mother to return so she could unload that thankless burden.

After the minister's introduction and the singing of "Amazing Grace," her father rose and walked slowly to the lectern. Turning around, he stared at the gathering with a vacant look in his eyes. If anything, he appeared worse than when she'd last seen him. The bags under his eyes were dark half-moons and even the creases at the side of his mouth seemed longer and deeper. He stared at his brother in a silent plea.

Uncle Steve, glancing in alarm at Nicky and Karina, was

getting to his feet when her father took a piece of paper from the inside pocket of his jacket, unfolded it, and smoothed it down on the lectern. Her uncle sat back down, wiped his brow.

Clearing his throat, James Bosko began, "Lisa was the best person I have ever known."

Karina passed her a tissue as he continued. "The day I first saw her, I knew she was the one," he said. "It wasn't just that she was beautiful, which she was, but she was fun and so full of life." He went on, describing their courtship and how family was the most important thing in the world to her because she was an only child whose parents were dead.

Nicky choked back a sob, her sympathy for him now a burning ache in her chest. Even though he looked tired and haggard, a light had come into his eyes and she realized the picture she had of her father—stern and stoic—was a fraction of his true self. He hadn't talked about his wife, or let his daughters talk about her in his presence, because of the depth of his hurt. Perhaps he hadn't remarried because, in his mind, no one could have measured up to Lisa Bosko.

So much about her father she hadn't understood. Karina's protectiveness now making sense, the shame of her own behavior rose like a suffocating thickness in her throat.

Fifteen minutes later, after her sister had played piano for the singing of "How Great Thou Art," they received condolences in a lineup at the back of the chapel, then went into a large reception room for lunch and coffee.

The detective, Cullen Fraser, wearing a dark gray suit that hung expertly from his big shoulders, caught her eye and nodded, then continued talking to a woman, a pretty blond whose hair was cut in a stylish bob that looked like every strand had been snipped separately. They stood close together and obviously knew each other quite well. Her stomach hardening, she looked away.

She spent a few minutes with Emily and Matt, then joined her father and Karina to receive condolences from people who hadn't been at the service. Only a few people were familiar and many, it seemed, hadn't even met her mother. One woman, whose husband had been Nicky's dentist growing up, patted her on the hand. "Your mother and I were friends all throughout high school. She was just such a lovely person. I feel so awful for you girls and your father."

Nicky shot her a tight smile and looked for an escape route. This woman, like some others in the room, had for years openly criticized her mother for abandoning the family. She glanced at her father, wondering what he thought of all this, especially since he'd had to endure so much more of it, but his expression betrayed no irritation. He was a better person than she was.

After several minutes, Emily came by with a sandwich and Nicky sat down in one of the chairs set up around the perimeter of the room. The ex-boyfriend, Jason, approached and sat down on the other side. The young girl was nowhere to be seen. Cullen Fraser was still talking to the woman, who looked vaguely familiar.

Jason said, "How are you making out?"

"I'm all right. You?"

"Busy." He gave a satisfied smile. "Dad's grooming me to take over the company."

"Great."

He said, "There's a lot to learn and I'm taking some accounting courses, but I think I'm up for the challenge." His father, one of the richest men in the county, ran a chain of supermarkets. The company had started with Jason's grandfather, but it wasn't until the second generation it really took off.

"I'm sure you are."

He slapped her playfully. "Sorry you didn't stick with me?"

Nicky resisted an urge to roll her eyes as Emily said, "Who's the girlfriend? Steal her straight from high school?"

Nicky bit her lip to stifle a smile. So she wasn't the only one who had noticed the girl's age. Looking at Jason now it was hard to imagine what she'd seen in him. He wasn't particularly good looking or smart or funny or kind. But he had paid attention to her and made her feel wanted. And he'd been a bad boy back then. That had been the bonus. It ended when they'd gotten caught for stealing and crashing a motorboat. His father had bailed him out, hiring the best lawyer in town. Her own father had decided enough was enough, and she'd done five months in a juvenile detention center.

Cullen Fraser was across the room, talking to Emily's fiancé, Matt. The blond was gone. Catching her eye, he stared at her in with razor-sharp intensity. It was crazy—not just the way he looked at her, but the way her stomach got all twisted in response.

Warmth creeping up her neck and into her face, she turned away in time to see Jason's father approach and rose to greet him. Allan Spidell took both hands in hers, leaned in to kiss her on the cheek. "I'm so sorry about your mother, Nicole."

A tall, stocky man with a red complexion and a puffy face, Allan Spidell had the look of a man who drank too much. He'd lost most of his hair, with just gray wisps clinging stubbornly to the sides of his head. But he still looked powerful and fit and she remembered he'd played football in university. Jason, who was taller and slimmer, had been a promising decathlete before drugs and girls lured him away.

She said, "It was nice of you to come. I was trying to remember earlier how long my mother worked for you."

"You've got me there. Two, three years?"

Nicky smiled. "She was a bookkeeper?"

"Right. She had a good mind for numbers. As well as being a lovely person." His eyes moistened.

She said, "I didn't realize you were close to her."

"We were good friends in high school."

She wanted to ask more questions, but he reached out and took her hands again. "I'm sorry, but I have to go. Take care." He gave a nod to Emily and his son, then left.

When he'd left, Nicky turned to Jason. "It's too bad he couldn't stay longer."

Jason said, "He and your father still don't get along." He must have caught a look of surprise on her face, because he said, "They haven't spoken since the court case."

Nicky wondered if there was more to it. She knew her father thought Jason should have been dealt with more harshly, but it hardly seemed worth holding a grudge over.

Jason leaned over, kissed her on the cheek, then stood up. "Want to get together some time?"

"That would be great," she heard herself say, realizing neither of them likely had any intention of following up on it.

A few minutes later, Emily and Matt left. Cullen Fraser was nowhere to be seen, she realized with a pang.

Karina, her father, and her uncle stood in a tight circle by the sandwich table. Nicky stood, walked toward them, then felt someone touch her arm. "Nicky?"

Turning around, she was face-to-face with a heavily pregnant woman in a purple dress. She couldn't remember the name of the woman, an acquaintance from high school. The woman said, "How are you?"

"I'm doing okay, all things considered."

"I am so sorry about your mom." She emphasized the word *so* and put her hand on Nicky's arm for added emphasis.

"Thank you." She nodded toward the woman's swollen belly. "I see congratulations are in order. When is the baby due?"

"Three weeks, not that I'm counting." She giggled, then seemed to remember herself and pinched her lips together. Moving in closer, her voice dropped to a whisper. "Do they have any idea who did it?"

Shaking her head, Nicky watched with increasing alarm as two more women walked toward them, maneuvering around the clutches of people. More people from high school, although these ones were not even acquaintances. She might have passed them in the hall. Their faces bore the too-eager expressions of people who were enjoying themselves. She held a coffee cup in front of her chest to stave off hugs.

They chatted for a few moments, with Nicky fending off questions first about the investigation and then increasingly intrusive ones about her personal life. No doubt curiosity about the wild child had been a motivating factor for them in attending the memorial. She could almost sense their disappointment, standing as she was before them, dressed formally in a white blouse, gray pencil skirt, and black pumps.

She glanced away, desperate now to escape. Karina was talking to her Uncle Steve and his ex-wife, Nola, who must have just arrived. Karina glanced in her direction, then back at Nola, seemingly oblivious to the desperation in her sister's eyes.

The three women had Nicky backed against a banquet table, determined to keep her captive. One of the women said, "Are you seeing anybody?" She was the biggest and tallest and had played basketball in high school.

"I'm going to steal Nicole, if you don't mind."

The deep voice came from behind the women. Smiling at them, Cullen reached in and grabbed her hand.

Nicky excused herself, but they were too busy looking at Cullen Fraser to take much notice of her. She followed him to the beverage table, where he poured a glass of water and handed it to her, taking her now mostly mangled coffee cup in exchange and depositing it on the table.

She took a long drink. "Thank you for that."

"You were looking pretty desperate."

"They wouldn't let me get away. A full-frontal charge would have been the only means of escape."

Up close it was obvious he'd had his hair trimmed. He glanced at the women, still huddled by the banquet table. "I can see why you didn't attempt it."

"Not very dignified behavior at a funeral."

He stroked her arm, gave her a little smile.

Even though she was at a memorial service, her mother's no less, the smile made her go a little weak in the knees. She was too vulnerable, too exposed around him.

She said, "It was very nice of you to come."

He didn't say anything, just continued looking at her.

Another thought came to her, this one even more inappropriate. If she could have mindless sex with somebody, he'd be a prime candidate.

Warmth crept up her neck and across her face. She took a large gulp of water, set the glass on the table, nodded at him, and walked away to join her family.

* * *

That night, after a dinner at her father's house of a warmed lasagna casserole, Nicky stacked the last plate in the dishwasher, gave the counter a final wipe, then joined her father, sister, and uncle in the family room.

Karina handed Nicky a glass of wine. "Thanks for cleaning up. I don't think I have an ounce of energy left in me. That was a very long day."

"It was the least I could do." Nicky smiled at her older sister, who'd been uncharacteristically withdrawn much of the day.

As Nicky sat down, her Uncle Steve said to her, "We were talking about what a nice service it was. Quite a few people came."

Nicky smiled and they chatted for a few minutes about people they hadn't seen in years who'd shown up, including a man and woman who'd been in the same medical school class as her father. The couple had flown in from California.

Her father said, his voice slightly slurred, "I didn't realize they'd married." Fatigue had deepened the lines of his face and his eyes were dull. He held his empty whiskey glass, his third, for Karina to refill.

Karina seemed about to say something, then rose to refill it. Her father waited until she'd sat down again, then said, "There were a lot of people I hadn't seen in years. I'm not sure I wanted to see some of them."

Nicky waited, tense.

Her father took a sip of whiskey, then looked at his daughters. "Some of them didn't have very nice things to say about your mother over the years."

"Daddy," Karina said, getting to her feet.

He held up a hand for her to stop. "You have a right to know. Your mother and I talked about this affair." A snarl curled his lips as he said the word "affair." "But it was over."

The raw tone in his voice knotting her stomach, Nicky glanced at Karina, who knelt in front of him, putting her hands on his knees. "Of course it was."

Pushing her hand away, he flopped back. His face was red and the slur was even more pronounced. A lump rose in Nicky's throat. It was the first time she'd seen him drunk. By the looks on their faces, Karina and her Uncle Steve shared her surprise.

After a tense silence, Karina got up and went back to her seat. Nicky was about to ask if anyone wanted coffee when her father said, "I'm not finished." His voice was harsh.

She froze. Her uncle stared grimly at his glass.

Karina said, "Take all the time you want, Dad. We want to hear." Long experience had obviously taught her not to interfere when their father was angry.

James Bosko drew in a sharp breath. "I forgave her and it didn't change the way I felt about her. Nothing could have changed the way I felt about her. She was my life." His eyes moistened with tears, which he brushed away. "But I won't forgive him because I know he killed her."

"Daddy—" Karina's voice was shaky.

Ignoring her, he stared at each of them in turn. "I don't know why he killed her, but I do know I have to find out who he is if it is the last thing I do." He broke down in sobs, joined quickly by Karina.

Biting at her lips, Nicky exchanged a glance with her uncle. His face had gone tomato red, as if he felt the pain just as much as her father.

After a few minutes, Nicky went into the kitchen to put coffee on. Everything, it seemed, had shifted. Their father, normally so taciturn, had opened up in a way she had never seen before. Part of it was the booze, but it seemed as if the murder hadn't just aged him but made him bitter.

The light had gone out of his eyes. They were glazed, cold.

Filling the coffee filter with grounds, she glanced at Karina, who was reclined on the sofa staring ahead, her eyes vacant. Tears filled Nicky's eyes. She hated to see her father and Karina like this.

Her uncle walked into the kitchen. "I feel helpless. I have no idea what to do." He spoke in a quiet tone.

"You and me both," she said, reaching into a cabinet for coffee mugs. "I feel like I should be doing more to help the police, but I can't seem to remember much from back then. Whatever's there is buried pretty deep. I get some snippets but nothing useful."

He grimaced. "You can't blame yourself. Even if you could remember, there's no telling it would have anything to do with what happened to your mother."

"I realize that." The doubt in her voice was poorly concealed and he reached over to stroke her arm. She poured coffee into the mugs and reached for a tray beside the toaster oven.

Her father had fallen asleep. Slumped to one side, eyes closed and mouth hanging open, his head bobbed forward on his neck. Beside him, Karina still had that dazed look.

Putting the mugs onto a tray, Nicky hesitated, feeling a heaviness in her body. For her whole life, her instinct had been to rebel and run away. The temptation now was stronger than ever. But running away was not an option. If she wanted to help her father, and Karina and herself, she had to carry her weight and help find out who killed her mother. Otherwise it might never be over.

Nothing could be done now about the hurt her behavior had caused her father in the past, but in this, at least, maybe she wouldn't disappoint him. Maybe she could earn a measure of redemption.

Picking up the tray, she followed her uncle into the family room.

CHAPTER EIGHT

It took Nicky just over an hour on Saturday morning to drive to Lisette, where she stopped at a service station and asked the teenaged boy behind the counter for directions to the farm where her mother's remains had been found. When she spotted the two-story house from the road thirty minutes later, she put her compact Chevy in second gear, drove quickly up the long, rutted lane, and then found a hard-packed surface near the house where she could park. The barn, or what was left of it, was a crumpled heap of boards one hundred yards farther down the lane.

The house wasn't anything like what she remembered. It wasn't white any more, the paint having peeled away to expose weathered-gray horizontal boards. Many of them had fallen off, offering glimpses right through the house to the trees and gray sky on the other side. Windows held no glass and a section of the moss-carpeted gabled roof had caved in, flattening the front porch.

Walking around the house to the back, a breeze whipped hair around her face. A tiny brown bird, likely a sparrow of some sort, flitted about a wild rose bush growing in the middle of the grass in what would have once been the backyard. Trampled grass seemed to indicate the house and immediate grounds had been searched, although there was no evidence of digging. The rear entrance to the house was an old wooden door with a rusty latch.

She came around the house full circle and stood beside the car. In the lane, muddy ruts from large tire tracks continued down to the barn. Hadn't Fraser and Ackerman mentioned the remains had been found near the barn? Swallowing hard, she hesitated a moment, then grabbed a sweater from the car and set off.

Yellow caution tape fluttered in the wind above a machine-dug hole near the barn's stone foundation. A large area had been excavated, roughly twelve square feet, the dirt dumped in small piles to the side. At some point, possibly as part of the police search, the barn had been flattened. The boards lay every which way in a pile about ten feet high on the far side of the foundation.

Had her mother been photographing the barn when she was killed? Or was she killed elsewhere on the property, the house maybe, then buried here?

Icy fingers grabbed her heart and squeezed. Suddenly feeling dizzy, she found a large rock and sat down. She shouldn't have come alone, should have taken Emily up on her offer to tag along.

The wind picked up and dark clouds blackened the sky.

Walking back to the car, she retrieved a water bottle and took a long drink. She'd had the vague notion coming here would make her feel better, which she now realized was ludicrous, although she could understand what had intrigued her mother. A derelict property held so many mysteries. How many generations had lived in it, and why had it been abandoned? How had her mother found it? Had the pictures she had surely taken here been destroyed?

The rain started coming down in earnest. Nicky pulled up her hood and dashed to the back door. So far, the farm had released no memories, but the inside might be different.

The latch on the back door was broken, allowing easy entry to a small room that would have served as a mudroom or back porch. A built-in cupboard occupied one wall, while another held five rusty hooks for coats. Through an open doorway was the kitchen at the front of the house. Fragments of plaster and empty tin cans littered the sloping floor. Shoe and boot prints in the dirt were evidence many people had walked on these floors recently. Cops.

Off the kitchen was where the center hallway had been, now a crumbling jumble of rotted boards from where the roof had caved in, taking the second story and front porch with it. Rain washed down through a gaping hole. A musty smell invaded her nose and mouth.

In the kitchen, against one wall, stood an enamel stove with a cast-iron top. An old straw broom, its bristles curled from use, gathered dust in a corner. Behind the stove, wallpaper in a large geometric pattern covered the wall. She walked over to look at it more closely, her shoes scuffing the dirt on the floor, and a memory rose suddenly. Closing her eyes, she brought it into focus. She had been in this room. Her mother had marveled at the wallpaper, a retro yellow-and-orange print now peeling away to expose large patches of crumbling plaster.

She clutched her chest as more memories and images tumbled through her mind. Her mother laughing. Taking pictures. The doll's carriage had been in the room across the hall, which wasn't accessible now. But she had crossed the hall all those years ago, and they had gone upstairs, she first, her mother following. Her mother had warned her to be careful. She remembered rooms with low, sloping ceilings, an old bed.

As she peered up through the hole, a sound came from outside. Someone was opening the back door.

* * *

Cullen opened the back door of the farmhouse. When he'd driven up the lane just minutes earlier, he'd spotted an old car parked beside the house. It was likely kids, teenagers. They had no business being here.

A headache sawed away at the area around his eyes. He massaged his temples, but there was no hope for it. He'd had too much to drink the night before and had only himself to blame.

Swinging the back door open, he glanced around the small room and listened for the intruders. Nothing, save the wind and rain. Stepping inside, he closed the door and walked into the kitchen.

A sudden movement caught his eye. It happened so quickly

he barely had time to react. He put his hand up to shield his head as something came swinging toward him. The object struck his hand. Grabbing it, he yelled out in pain and a woman screamed.

Nicole Bosko.

Staring at the broom handle in his hand, he cursed loudly.

Her whole body shaking, she stared at him with bulging eyes. Then she slumped against the wall and covered her face. Speech must have been impossible, because if she'd been able to talk, he'd be hearing it.

His pulse raced. "What the hell are you doing here?"

She stood rigid against the wall, nostrils flaring, still saying nothing. With shaking hands, she pushed strands of wet hair from her face. Her mouth was agape, exposing chattering white teeth.

She was terrified. He took a step toward her.

She held up her hand to stop him from coming closer. Her breaths were short and raspy and it was a long moment before she spoke. "What am *I* doing here? I'd say the question is more what are *you* doing here?"

"I'd think that was very obvious. I'm investigating a murder."

"You said the police were finished here."

"Officially, yes, I came to see if I missed something. You?"

She said, "I came to see if I could remember anything."

"That's great. I'm glad you're trying to remember stuff, but I don't think it's a good idea to come alone." For someone who was obviously smart, she didn't seem to act like it. Her mother had been killed here, for God's sake.

When she didn't say anything, he said, "Well?"

Those dark eyes shot daggers at him. "Well what? You didn't ask a question."

"Do you remember anything?"

"I remember being here with my mother, but not much else." She pinched her lips together. "I'm sorry about almost clobbering you. I didn't realize it was you."

He propped the broom against the wall. "Maybe next time you should check first."

Ignoring the comment, she walked across the room and looked out the kitchen window, fingered a piece of gauzy fabric, browned with age, hanging from a thin metal curtain rod. She was wearing a hoodie and skinny jeans that showed off a cute butt and her long legs.

He looked away, feeling the heat rising in his neck, and walked toward the center hallway, where he could see dark sky through a hole in the roof.

She said, "So?"

He shook his head, stifled a yawn. "So what?"

"So have you missed anything? Or are you too tired?"

"I've only just gotten here." The words came out gruff. Her attitude didn't help. Or that the three cups of coffee he'd had on the drive over pooled like acid in his gut.

"Well, I'll leave you to it, then." Rubbing her hands together, she gave the room a once-over, then walked toward the back porch.

He didn't want her to leave. "Wait."

She turned around, raised one of those arched eyebrows. He'd never seen eyes as dark as hers, more black than brown.

He said, "Make sure you have a good look around, in case you can remember anything."

"I've had a good look, so if you don't mind, I'll leave you to it."

He rubbed his temples, a tight band of pressure now encircling his head. This was not going well and he realized it never would. He was attracted to a woman who couldn't stand the sight of him.

She said, "One thing before I go. Was this place searched when she first went missing?"

"No, apparently, nobody mentioned it at the time. And you're the only one who says they remember coming here with her. Your father says he didn't know about it. Maybe she thought he would disapprove."

Her eyebrows shot up. "Why would he disapprove?"

He gestured around the room. On the counter beside the enamel sink, an old jar held two wooden spoons and a rusted spatula. In the middle of the ceiling, a bare lightbulb hung from a frayed cord. Filling the air was a smell of decay and emptiness. "It's not everybody's cup of tea."

"I remember I loved it. It was mysterious. Even now it makes me wonder about the people who lived here, how many families. Now it will be torn down and all new houses put up." Sadness replaced the anger in her eyes. "There will be a new layer of history, and all the secrets of the past will be buried. Including what happened to my mother."

The comment surprised him, not the sentiment so much as her sharing it.

She said, "Was it thoroughly searched after my mother's

body was found?" At his nod, she said, "No camera was found?"

He shook his head. "We checked everywhere."

She said, "The house is a lot smaller than I remembered. In my mind it was more like a mansion."

"Sometimes when you're little, you think everything's big."

"True."

If anything, she was more beautiful today, her oval face slightly flushed, the damp hair falling over her shoulders like rain. And of course those deep, dark eyes.

He smiled. "Well, at least we have found something to agree on."

"I wouldn't let it go to your head."

The remark itself wasn't bad, but the scornful smile accompanying it had him clenching his jaw. He said, "You really should learn to hold your tongue."

Her eyebrows shot up. She was goading him and it was as if she enjoyed doing it, was making a sport of it, even. "What's that supposed to mean?"

He said, "I think the statement was pretty clear. You're so busy being angry at me you can't see past that, even if it would help solve your mother's murder."

"I get it." She glanced at him scornfully. "You're going to blame me if you don't solve this case. You should stop harassing me and look for some real clues."

"Don't tell me how to do my job. I know how to do my job."

"If that were the case, you would already know who killed my mother. You certainly wouldn't be wasting your time trying to dig up the old memories of a messed-up kid."

He scoffed. "I don't think you were a messed-up kid, and you're certainly not a messed-up adult. What you are is a woman who is so afraid of people caring about her that you'd rather hold on to childhood anger than allow somebody to help you."

Eyes narrowed, she crossed the floor to stand directly in front of him. "How dare you. You know nothing about me."

"I know that I care about you."

For a second, her looked softened, and then she was angry again. "I think you're trying to blame me for your failings. If you don't solve this, it won't be because of me. It'll be because you've been out drinking late and you're too hungover to do your job properly. Or because you're having girlfriend troubles or something. You've got that look about you."

His pulse ratcheted up. That remark hit too close to home.

She turned to go and he reached out and grabbed her, pulling her to him. Before he even knew what he was doing, he was kissing her.

* * *

Nicky slammed her palms against Cullen Fraser's chest and shoved him away. Her heart hammered against her ribs. She glared at him, too shocked to contemplate how her body was reacting to him kissing her and what she felt about it.

A flush crept across Cullen's cheeks. He looked down, then backed up and stood against the wall of the kitchen next to the window.

Running his hands through his hair, he looked more than

a little disheveled. Outrageously good looking, his light blue T-shirt—no logo today—form fitting enough to outline the muscles of his chest and arms. His eyes were on her again. Really, it should be against the law for a man to look like that—and to look at a woman the way he was looking at her, as if he wanted to eat her.

Heat flooded her, sweeping up her neck and into her face. She glanced at the door. Now would be a good time to leave. A strong instinct for self-preservation told her to get out. It was like a warning light at a railroad crossing with a freight train barreling down the tracks.

The kiss had been hard and brutal, like a punishment. Here was a guy who had to have control, and she couldn't take anybody telling her what to do. Not to mention the girlfriend. She could tell by his reaction to her remark about girlfriend troubles the blond was in the picture.

Yes, it was all so very wrong.

He cleared his throat. "I'm sorry," he said, his voice thick.

Not saying anything, she turned and walked quickly out of the kitchen, yanked open the back door, and ran across the damp grass to her car. In the car, she turned the key in the ignition and the wipers thumped across the windshield, washing away squiggly lines of rain.

A knuckle knocked on the window. She took in a breath, then another, then reached over and cranked down the window halfway. Stared straight ahead. He was likely wondering how much trouble he was in, whether she would tell his boss. She should. But it would be her word against his, and she knew how that would go.

"I'm sorry," he said.

"You already said that." Glancing at him, she noticed a little scar above his lip, barely visible under his moustache. Realizing there was no future for them, she could regard him with an almost clinical detachment. Even admit he ticked one of her boxes. She liked a man who didn't hold back and it was clear he was one of those.

He said, "I just wanted you to know I meant that I was sorry and I don't know why I kissed you."

Putting the car in reverse, she glared at him in silence for a moment, then said, "I do."

He waited.

"Because you're an obnoxious asshole," she said with grim satisfaction.

CHAPTER NINE

On Monday, Nicky started back at work. Her boss had offered more time off but she'd declined, figuring it would be good to focus on something other than her mother's murder and her own grief.

The shelter was busy, as Mondays tended to be, with three admissions, an eighteen-year-old boy transferred from an adult shelter and later sixteen-year-old twin sisters who'd been living in a car with their abusive mother. Finding a school close to the shelter willing to take the transfer took a couple of hours. But the day passed quickly and before she knew it, it was time to leave.

Straight after work she drove out to visit her uncle, whose house was six miles farther up the lake road from her father's place. He'd phoned that morning to invite her for supper with him and his ex-wife. Nola Bosko had moved to a house in Riverdale after the divorce, but they were still friends.

Nola answered the door. In the kitchen, her uncle sat at

a granite-topped island reading a magazine. Nola got a soda from the refrigerator for Nicky, then grabbed ingredients to make a salad. They talked for a few minutes about Nicky's return to work and Nola's plans to cut back on her hours as a building inspector. Her uncle went outside and fired up the barbecue, but it wasn't until they were at the dining table and nearly finished eating that they revealed the reason for the invitation.

Nola put her fork on her plate with a clinking sound, then pushed it away. "I'm not sure if you're interested, but I have a few albums of photos your mother took."

Nicky nodded encouragement but her aunt was looking off to the side. She had a disconcerting habit of avoiding eye contact when talking to people. It didn't seem to be shyness, but coupled with her formal manner, it always managed to set Nicky on edge.

A brief glance, then Nola averted her eyes. "She gave them to me many years ago. I was wondering if you would like to have them."

Smiling, Nicky sat forward. "I'd love to have them. But what about my father and Karina? Did you ask them?"

Nola exchanged a look with her former husband, and it seemed obvious they had discussed this. He said, "Of course, it's up to you to do with them as you will, but you seemed the obvious choice. It's just you remind us so much of your mother."

"I appreciate that." She smiled at Nola. "Were you close to my mother?"

Her ears turned pink and she turned to her ex-husband,

who said, "We were all close at one time, but we sort of drifted apart." He cleared his throat. "I suppose life just got in the way. Both your father and I got busy at work and of course he started going on relief missions soon after you were born."

His tight smile suggested there was more to the story. Karina had once said her aunt and uncle hadn't been able to have children. That might have added strain. It seemed there was so much about her family that was a mystery to her.

Nola stood up. "Well, that's settled, then. I'm going to clean up. You two stay and chat." She flicked a brief glance at Nicky. "No matter what happened, we have fond memories of your mother."

No matter what happened? Nicky tensed. It seemed an odd thing to say, unless she was simply referring to Lisa Bosko's murder.

Gathering the plates, Nola continued, "She was a free spirit, an independent thinker, artistic."

Her uncle pushed his chair away from the table, its legs scraping the tile floor. "You remind us a lot of her. We were talking about that earlier."

Warmth tugged at her heart. "Thank you." That she'd resembled her mother beyond the physical was something she hadn't heard before.

Nola said, "In many ways, your mother was the opposite of your father, which I suppose was why they suited each other so well. Not that he isn't caring, I don't mean that. But he's a type A, like me. Your mom was much more relaxed. She made sure you had fun."

"I do remember having fun," Nicky said as Nola turned

away. She turned to her uncle. "I wanted to ask you something. Do you have any idea who my mother was having an affair with?"

He shook his head.

She said, "Maybe she threatened to leave him and he was angry enough to kill her because of that."

"It's possible, but…" He let the sentence trail off.

"How close was she to Allan Spidell? I talked to him at the memorial service, and he mentioned they were friends."

"I suppose you could say that. They never dated, if that's what you're asking. But they were part of a group of us that hung out together in high school."

"And after? When she came back to Riverton after university?"

Stiffening, he twisted an engineering class ring on his finger. "I don't think the friendship continued. Your mother married your father soon after she returned. She did go to work for Allan for a while, but if you're suggesting she had anything to do with him, I think you're off the mark."

She reached out and touched his arm. The question had clearly upset him. "I'm not suggesting anything of the sort. I was just curious."

"Of course, I'm sorry. I guess we're all a bit touchy. But Allan was not her type at all. There's a side to him you don't want to see."

"What side?"

He picked up a salt shaker, set it back down. "He had a bit of a reputation back then as something of a lothario. Your mother saw through that. And now he's got a different reputation. Rumors suggest he's mixed up in some shady business stuff."

Nicky mulled this over, wondered how far back the business problems went. Was it possible Allan Spidell had coerced her mother, as his bookkeeper, into doing something she hadn't wanted to do? Did the police have Spidell on their radar?

Getting up, her uncle walked to the sliding doors. Just off the patio, a large blue tarp covered the in-ground swimming pool in preparation for winter. Hands in his pockets, he turned back to her. "Your father partly blames himself. He thinks maybe your mother wasn't happy, and he didn't realize it. He feels guilty about that."

The sadness in his eyes made her chest ache, not just for her father, who blamed himself when there was no blame to be had, but for her uncle, weighed down by helplessness. Joining him at the window, she stroked his arm and tried to think of something to say but came up short and decided not to say anything.

She glanced behind her. Nola met her eyes for the briefest of moments, then looked away.

* * *

On Wednesday, Nicky met with Emily and her fiancé, Matt, after work at a new pizzeria a couple of blocks from the shelter. They were sitting in a booth at the back when she arrived. Soft pop music played in the background and the lighting was dim.

"Sorry I'm late." She slid into the booth and put her shoulder bag and another bag on the seat beside her, then looked at each of them in turn. "You two look like the cat that ate the canary. What's up?"

Matt grinned at Emily. "We're getting married in November, right before my mother takes off for Europe."

"Wow." She stood up, leaned across the table, and kissed them both. They were so much in love it was hard not to be enthusiastic for them. "Wonderful. Am I invited?"

Emily rolled her eyes. "Of course. It will be here, in Riverton." Emily and Matt were living in Boston, where Matt worked and Emily went to law school. Matt was in Riverton consulting with an architect on a design for houses he hoped to build on infill lots.

Matt said, "We would have done it sooner, but I was waiting for Emily's hair to grow out."

This earned a playful punch from Emily. "It's going to be low-key, although I will need help shopping for a wedding dress."

Nicky winced. "Not sure I'm the best person. I'm not exactly girly."

"And I am?" Emily smirked. "Don't worry. Between the two of us we should be able to come up with something decent, don't you think?" She turned to her fiancé, her eyes glowing. "What do you think, Matt?"

He didn't miss a beat. "I was never much one for decent. I'll be more interested in seeing you out of the dress than in it."

Emily shook her head in mock horror as the waiter came with their pizzas, setting an oozing mess of smoked mozzarella, pancetta and pureed squash in front of Nicky. She took a bite while Emily related more details about the wedding. It wasn't hard to see that Emily, who'd been through such a tough time, had her act together.

"Is your mother coming?"

"Oh, yeah. It took some talking, but she'll come."

"What was the problem?" Her pizza was savory and sweet, the crust charred to perfection.

"She wanted Frank, her boyfriend, to walk me down the aisle."

Matt grimaced. "Emily told her mother she didn't need anybody to walk her down the aisle, and then the shit hit the fan. But we stuck to our guns and she seems okay with it now."

Nicky kept a poker face. "Ask your mom to help you find a wedding dress. That would really make it up to her."

Emily did a double-take. "Are you kidding?"

Nicky's lips curled into a grin. "Of course I am."

Matt said, "We're getting her to look after the venue. We figure it'll keep her happy."

Nicky's cell phone, which she had put on the table in front of her, vibrated with an incoming call. She glanced at the number, thought about answering it, and decided to wait.

Emily looked at her expectantly.

"My sister," she said. "I'll call her later."

Matt said, "Are you close to your sister?"

She chose her words carefully. "I wouldn't describe our relationship as close."

Emily said, "She's five years older, right?"

Nicky nodded. "The age difference has something to do with it, sure, but it was mostly my own doing. We had a big rivalry when we were younger. I resented that she was better at everything and was allowed to do things like stay up later. Of course, she was older so it made sense."

He said, "I had something similar with my sister. Now I can understand it, but at the time it was maddening."

The waiter cleared their dishes away and they ordered coffee. Nicky got out the three photo albums Nola had given her. She'd been through them the previous night but wanted to show Matt, who was an amateur photographer.

She opened the first album. "I'm not sure what I expected to see. I guess I'd hoped they'd reveal some hidden secret that would unlock this whole mystery, but I don't think so."

Matt had flipped through several pages. "They're stunning, Nicky. Your mother had quite an eye."

Many of the photographs were architectural. She recognized Riverton's old library, shot from an angle on a rainy day with gloomy clouds looming in the sky. Matt pointed to a winter shot of an open field with a single leafless tree standing like a skeleton in the background. A single set of boot prints starting from where her mother, the photographer, stood led across virgin snow to the tree about a hundred yards in the distance.

He said, "It's simple, but that's what makes it so striking."

Emily leaned over to examine the photograph. "I agree. It's got a wistful quality, hasn't it? But it's a bit mysterious, too. It makes you wonder who made the boot prints. Your mother obviously didn't, because you don't see the return prints."

Nicky took another look. "That's odd, now that you mention it. Maybe he or she is hiding behind the tree. It wasn't me; the boots are too big." She wondered if the photo held an important clue and hairs stood up on the back of her neck. "I'll have to ask my father if he has any idea."

Many of the pictures were of abandoned buildings and rural landscapes. Some were simple, like a decaying house in a field, or a close-up of an abandoned farm with overgrown shrubs, shot through overhanging branches, its windows broken, paint peeling, front door open. Photos of interiors, too, old doors, living rooms, sometimes with couches still in them. In one, three bottles of prescription medication stood on a windowsill; in another, a porcelain doll lay on a bedroom floor, eyes open, missing an arm, its burgundy dress in tatters. None appeared to be from the farmhouse.

Emily pointed to a picture of an old staircase. Nicky's mother had stood at the bottom of the stairs. A wooden railing drew the eye upward to an open door at the top, providing a glimpse into a green room with a sunlit window.

"It's eerie," Emily said. "Kind of creepy with the peeling paint on the walls, but it makes you wonder who lived there, why they left, and what kind of lives they led. You get the feeling their ghosts still live there. Not a place to go alone."

Nicky shuddered. "I have a feeling I've been in some of these places." She pointed to a photo of a large room in an institutional-style building. "Like this one. It looks like it used to be a hospital. I'll check online later to see if I can find it."

Nicky finished her last slice of pizza and wiped her mouth with a napkin. As beautiful as the photos were, they didn't seem to hold any clues about what had happened to her mother.

Matt left shortly after to meet with the architect, promising to pick Emily up at Nicky's place, which was a fifteen-minute walk from the pizzeria. Outside, on the sidewalk, Nicky slipped into her cardigan. Dusk was closing in and there was a chill in the air.

They'd walked for a minute in silence when Emily punched her arm playfully. "You're holding back."

"What are you talking about?"

"The cop, Nicky. I saw him at your mom's memorial service." At Nicky's blank look, Emily said, "You never told me he looked like that."

"It doesn't matter what he looks like. He's a jerk."

Two teenage boys came up behind them on skateboards, expertly swerving around them. They stopped at a convenience store, tucked the boards under their arms, and went inside.

Emily said, "He couldn't keep his eyes off you."

She shrugged. "That's me, a regular hunk magnet. But, seriously, I have no interest in him." At Emily's raised eyebrows, she said, "Something I did want to ask you about though. I saw him talking to Matt. Did they know each other beforehand?"

"They just met recently. Apparently, this cop's ex-girlfriend introduced them. She works in TV and she interviewed Matt once about something or other."

"The blond? I thought I recognized her."

"That's her. Anyway, Matt was quite impressed with this Cullen Fraser. Said he seemed quite intelligent."

It was Nicky's turn to raise her eyebrows. "So?"

Emily smiled. "So, you like the smart ones. And not all men are jerks."

"He's just a bit too intense for me."

"Maybe it's you that makes him intense."

She rolled her eyes. "Whatever. Anyway, he's not my type."

"Nobody'd be your type if you had a choice."

"What's that supposed to mean?"

"Well, what would be your type, then?"

She thought about it for a moment.

Emily said, "My point exactly. You're not exactly the best at opening up to people. Not that it isn't understandable, given your family history and everything, but maybe he's worth a chance."

CHAPTER TEN

Parked for over an hour outside the Stevens Youth Shelter on Thursday, Cullen Fraser kept his eye on the front door until Nicole Bosko finally appeared just after six p.m. A gust of wind tossed her hair around her face and she reached up to brush it away before starting down the steps. When she spotted the car, she hesitated a moment, then stepped forward.

Cullen reached over and opened the door. "Want a ride?" he said, adding when she made no move, "I wanted to update you on the investigation."

Raising her eyebrows, she got in and put her handbag on her lap. She was wearing dark jeans and an oversized coffee-colored sweater. She looked like a million bucks, her skin soft and flawless, her hair silky. His stomach clenched.

He cleared his throat. "Everything okay between us?"

Eyes narrowed, she said, "What do you mean?"

She obviously wasn't going to make it easy, which shouldn't have been a surprise. "I'm talking about the other day."

"You already apologized. Let's just forget about it, okay?" She stared straight ahead. "I thought you wanted to update me on your investigation."

"I just wanted to make sure we're okay."

"I'm not going to report you, if that's what you're worried about. Can you just drive me home?"

Being reported hadn't been his worry so much as correcting her impression he was a total jerk. Which he had been. But he wasn't. Usually.

He pulled into traffic, drove to the end of the block, and hung a right. "Thank you, but I also wanted to say I'm not an asshole."

"What about obnoxious? I distinctly remember calling you an obnoxious asshole. Are you admitting to being obnoxious?" The barest hint of amusement lit her eyes.

"I always thought they were one and the same."

This time, the spark in her eyes was accompanied by a slight smile on those luscious lips. "I suppose you're right."

His heart did a little flip and he wanted to touch her so badly it hurt, to trace his hand up her arm and across her face. What was up with that? He was acting like lovesick schoolboy.

He said, "By the way, I know about the runaway."

She tensed. "What are you talking about?"

"Michelle. The girl you were with the day you ran from me."

Her eyes widened. "Don't worry, I'm not here about her. I have no interest in bringing her in, if that's what you're worried about. But if you'd told me you were worried about her, instead of just complaining about police harassment in general, we would have saved a whole lot of trouble."

Relief relaxed her face. "I couldn't risk it; I wasn't sure how you or your partner would react. I know he's not a Riverton cop. I guess I thought there might be pressure. Besides, it's kind of a murky area, legally speaking."

"How is she doing?"

"She's all right. She's actually been moved to foster care while some more permanent arrangement is set up. Apparently, there's an aunt she…" She let the sentence drop off, as if she realized she'd already told him too much.

"Don't worry. My lips are sealed. I don't want to see kids sent back into bad homes no matter who their fathers are. I'm glad to hear things are working out."

For a minute, neither of them said anything. He got the feeling she didn't do small talk, and he wasn't so great at it, either. There was a tension in the car, like weird currents pulling in different ways.

They were coming up to her street when she said, "Do you have any leads yet?"

"We're following up on several things." Not quite a lie, but it wasn't the full truth either. He just didn't want to tell her the chances of solving this cold case were slim. That they'd spent hours checking up on her father and even more time trying to track the elusive mystery man who had apparently been Lisa Bosko's one-time lover.

"Like what?"

"Two other women went missing at the same time as your mother. One of the bodies was recovered two weeks after she went missing, in a park. The other woman's body was never found."

She paled. "Was anybody ever charged?"

He shook his head. "The woman whose body was found died of a single bullet wound. She was thirty-eight, divorced. Police suspected her boyfriend but they couldn't prove anything and he was never charged. He's in prison in California serving life for murdering two pharmacists in a drugstore robbery."

"Do you think there's a connection with my mother?"

"It's too early to say. We're checking his alibi for the time your mother went missing and he's being interviewed in prison tomorrow. I'll fill you in when I find out how that went."

She shivered. "I realize it's not your fault, but it doesn't sound hopeful, does it?"

He pinched his lips together, debating whether to come straight with her. "Cold cases can be difficult but there's still hope. I was pulled off the case this week for two days to look into another homicide."

"The university student?"

He nodded. On Tuesday, a fourth-year chemistry student who sold marijuana to help fund his education had been murdered during a drug deal. This morning, they'd charged one of his clients, another university student, with murder.

She said, "But you're still working on my mother's case?"

"When I can, yes. I won't give up."

She inhaled shakily. "Thank you."

A minute later, he pulled up in front of her apartment building.

"Thank you." She was about to open the door, then turned to him. "Would you like to come up for coffee? Or a sandwich? That's all I can offer. I don't have anything planned for supper. There's something I wanted to ask you about."

Even though he knew this was strictly professional, his heart did that funny flip again. Signs suggested a thawing of her attitude toward him. "Why don't we just go somewhere so you don't have to bother?"

She studied him a moment, then shook her head. "I was out last night and to tell you the truth, I don't feel up to it. Plus, I don't have much of an appetite."

"A sandwich is fine."

Inside, he made coffee while she made ham and cheese sandwiches. They sat in the living room, balancing plates on their laps. The room had been decorated on the cheap, but it felt warm and welcoming.

She said, "Did you know my mother used to work for Allan Spidell?"

"The guy who owns the grocery stores?"

"She worked as his bookkeeper for a couple of years. He was at the memorial last week, but he didn't stay long. He's a big guy, sort of stocky, tall."

"I remember. Was that his son you were talking to?"

"Jason Spidell, yes. We have a history." She took a bite of her sandwich. "Anyway, about his father, he mentioned he was a friend of my mother's. And Jason told me his dad and my father had a falling out."

"What it was about?"

"I think it goes back to when Jason and I were teenagers. We got in trouble."

"Jason led you down a wayward path?"

"Not at all. I led myself. We stole a motorboat and went for a joyride. We'd both been drinking. We crashed. The boat was totaled. Jason was driving, but I was a willing participant in the ride. He didn't force me."

"But neither of you was hurt, which is the main thing, as the cliché goes." That she hadn't been hurt suddenly cheered him.

"The thing is, Jason's father made sure Jason got off scot-free, whereas my father'd had enough of my hijinks and was more than happy to let the judge send me to detention."

"Doesn't sound fair."

She thought for a moment. "In the end, my father might have done me a favor. Jason ended up doing a stint in jail."

"What for?"

"He got in a fight in a restaurant and smashed a chair over somebody's head. I don't know any more details. It was a few years back and I think he's doing okay these days." She took a sip of coffee, set the mug down on the table. "But I didn't ask you up here to talk about me or Jason. I just wanted to fill you in on Allan Spidell. Maybe the trouble between him and my father started when Jason and I got into trouble, because my father thought Jason should have had the book thrown at him. But maybe it started earlier."

Cullen made a mental note to pay Spidell a visit. "You mean back to when your mother was alive and working for Allan Spidell?"

"It's possible, isn't it? I just thought you might want to check it out."

He nodded and she got up, picked up the dirty plates, and carried them into the kitchen. When she came back, she said, "Regardless of what you think of me, I've put those days behind me."

He bristled. "How do you know what I think of you?"

"You're right. That was unfair." She sat down. "And you? Can I ask why you became a cop?"

"A lot of reasons. But when I was a teenager—mostly obeying the law, by the way—a friend's older sister went missing. She was in high school, working part time at a hardware store. She finished her shift, said good-bye to her coworkers, walked out into the parking lot, and was never heard from again. Three years later, her father died of a heart attack. He went to his grave not knowing what happened to his daughter."

He could still picture her, tall and skinny, nicknamed Ginger because of her red hair, smart as a whip, focused on school. A face he'd never forget.

Tears stained her eyes. "I'm sorry. But from what I've been reading there are lots of those stories."

A sudden heaviness weighed on his chest. It was true. In many cases, families never got answers. He wanted desperately to find answers for Nicole, but would he be able to? He looked away, unsure of what to say.

She wiped her eyes. "In some ways I think I would have been better off not knowing my mother was dead."

Despair darkening her eyes, she slumped forward and put her face in her hands and he had no trouble picturing the little girl in her, the one who had waited many years for her mother to come back before finally giving up. All the while raised by a father, already overworked, who was forced to raise two young daughters by himself.

Her stumbling along the way to adulthood wasn't hard to understand.

CHAPTER ELEVEN

Allan Spidell's horse ranch was about twenty-five miles east of Riverton, near a small town called Taunton Lake. Nicky had always thought the name odd, since there was no lake within miles of the town. There was a river, the Sutton, which the road met up with five miles outside of Taunton Lake. Slow and brackish, the river resembled a dark rope uncoiled across the green farm fields.

Just before the town limits, Nicky drove past a new subdivision, where half a dozen houses were under construction in a treeless field, then spotted the Spidell ranch on a hill in the distance. Allan Spidell had once joked he'd built on the hill so he could see his enemies coming, but she suspected it had more to do with a desire to display his wealth.

She turned off the road onto a long gravel driveway that curved back and forth as it mounted the hill. The house, built thirty years ago, was in the style of a traditional farmhouse, although with exaggerated columns and a curved front entry that someone must have thought a good idea at the time.

Jason answered the door. "Nicky, surprised to see you." He stepped aside, grinned. "Surprised but delighted."

They walked into the kitchen, where a woman who couldn't have been much older than Nicky sat at a stool at an oversized island.

Jason said, "Nicky, have you met Melanie? The new Mrs. Spidell?" The smirk accompanying the introduction suggested they weren't best of friends, but you could never be sure with Jason. She supposed he lived here, which shouldn't have come as too much of a surprise.

Standing, Melanie shook her hand. "I'm sorry about your mother." The way that she said it made it sound like she wasn't just being polite.

"Thank you. Had you met my mother?" Melanie would have been quite young, but it was possible.

"No, but Allan talked about her and I've been paying attention to the news. And I lost my mother when I was quite young. The circumstances weren't as tragic, but still."

"I'm sorry to hear that." On closer look, Nicky realized Melanie was older than she had first appeared, maybe in her mid- to late-thirties. She had little lines between her brows and crow's feet around her eyes, suggesting she smiled a lot. She had a healthy, tanned complexion, as if she spent a lot of time outdoors, and jeans and a chambray shirt reinforced that impression.

Melanie said, "Have you had lunch?"

Nicky declined. The kitchen had been updated in the decade since she'd been here, and it had dark wood cabinets, sleek appliances, and miles of granite countertop.

Melanie sat back down at the island, tucked into a half-eaten sandwich.

Jason cleared his throat. "Have you come to see me?"

Melanie rolled her eyes and Nicky realized she hadn't been wrong about the tension. These two did not get along.

She smiled at Melanie, warming to the third Mrs. Spidell. "I came to see your husband, actually. Is he here?"

"Let me call him. He shouldn't be too far away." Melanie picked up a cell phone off the counter. He must have answered the phone, because she explained the reason for the call, listened for a moment, and hung up. "He's at the stables. You'll have to drive. Just follow the road for a minute and you'll see it on the right."

Jason was leaning against a wall. "Do you want me to take you?"

Thanking her, Nicky turned to Jason. "I should be able to find it."

The stable was a big timber-frame structure a few minutes' drive down the lane. It looked new and expensive, with cedar siding and a silver metal roof. A riding ring out front looked new, too.

She parked behind a pickup truck at the side of the lane, just past a gate leading to a large fenced field where five horses grazed. A chestnut foal with a black tail peeked from behind its mother's dark flanks.

Walking up to the stable's set of heavy double doors, she used both hands to roll one to the side and entered. The smell of cedar, mixed with the sweet smell of hay and manure, filled the air. Beams crisscrossed the high vaulted ceiling. She called out but heard no answer so walked up the wide center aisle. A dozen stalls, six on each side, stood empty.

About to call out again, she heard a noise. Whipping her head around, she saw Allan Spidell standing in the shadows, watching her. Carrying a saddle on his arm, he must have just come out of the tack room.

"You scared me," she said, her hand at her chest.

"Hello there." Allan Spidell put the saddle on a rack, then walked over to shake her hand. He wore a thick gold necklace with a horseshoe pendant and as he got closer, she picked up the sour smell of alcohol on his breath.

She looked around. "This looks new."

"We've been doing a lot of work. We just finished this barn in the spring. Last year we put in a half-mile training track and the year before we added another pond."

"Impressive." If he had money worries, they weren't in evidence here.

"Melanie, my wife—did you meet Melanie?—she's been around horses her whole life. She's giving riding lessons and we're going to start boarding."

Nicky smiled. He spoke with some pride, his chest thrust out and his chin high. Again, she was aware of a kind of brutish power. He'd always struck her as a man who wouldn't let anything get in the way of what he wanted.

He said, "Was there something you wanted to see me about? If it's horse-related, you've come to the right place." He chuckled.

"I just came to talk about my mother, to see what else you can tell me about her."

"You're the spitting image of her, I can tell you that much." He ran his hand along the side board of a stall. "I was fond of her. I'm sorry I couldn't stay very long after the service."

"Jason says you and my dad don't get along."

"True, unfortunately. But what can you do?" He shrugged.

She prodded. "Was it to do with what happened with Jason and me?"

He nodded.

She said, "You'd think it would all be water under the bridge by now."

"With your father, it's never water under bridge. Never will be." Shrugging again, he took off the ball cap on his head, slapped it against his thigh, and then put it back on. "I'm too old to worry about getting along with your father."

"Did you ever date my mother?"

He stiffened, instantly defensive. "What makes you ask that?"

She shrugged, tried to act casual. "Just curious. I was young when my mom disappeared. I'm just trying to find out more about her."

He relaxed. "We were friends throughout school, your mother, me, your Uncle Steve and a few others, but we drifted apart when we graduated from high school. Her friendship with me never crossed the line. Not by choice on my part, I might add. Your mother had her heart set on somebody else." He picked up a broom, swept around the front of a stall. "Then your mom came back to Riverton, after college, and your father swept her off her feet."

"How'd she come to work for you?"

"She applied for a bookkeeping job."

"Did you hire her personally?"

He nodded. "But it wasn't any kind of nepotism. She was the most qualified candidate. Your mother was very smart."

"Why'd she quit?"

Frowning, he chewed the inside of his cheek. "I'm not sure. It wasn't long before she took off." He cleared his throat. "Sorry, what everybody thought at the time was her taking off. Maybe a month or two. She wouldn't say. I thought maybe she just wanted to spend more time at home. I thought she enjoyed the job, but there was nothing I could do to change her mind."

"It seems odd that she would quit to spend more time at home, considering I was going to school that fall."

He shrugged. "Beats me."

She met his gaze calmly. "Did you have an affair with my mother?"

For a moment, he just looked at her, as if he hadn't heard her correctly then he clenched his fists around the broom and stepped toward her. In an instant, his friendly manner had vanished, replaced by a barely contained rage.

He said, "Jesus, no. Where the hell did you get that from?" All trace of warmth was gone from his voice.

Heart pounding, she stumbled back, remembering Jason had once told her about his father's anger, how it came out of nowhere. She'd suspected Jason had been exaggerating, but now realized he hadn't been.

She said, "It was just a question. I didn't mean anything by it. You said yourself my mother was nice looking."

Her heart raced and her palms felt sweaty. Anger flashed in his eyes and she wondered if she'd made a big mistake coming here. The situation seemed to be sliding out of control. She tried to remember if she'd shut the door when she came in the stables. She figured she could outrun him to the door, but if it was closed, her chances of opening it and getting out before he caught her were highly questionable.

"Well, it's a hell of a question." Holding the broom with both hands across the front of his body, he took another step toward her. Red spots had appeared on his face and his lips curled into a snarl. "I have no idea what you're trying to pull, but I want you to get off my property. If you're looking for someone to blame for your mother's murder, I suggest you look elsewhere. I had nothing to do with it."

Taking a step back, she said in a shaky voice, "I'm sorry."

His knuckles on the broom handle were white. "I didn't have an affair with your mother and I would never have hurt her. You're trying to cause trouble for me, and it's the last thing I need. Now get out."

CHAPTER TWELVE

Smells good," Anna Ackerman said as Cullen plunked a large paper bag of Chinese food on her desk. It was seven p.m. on Monday night, the beginning of the fourth week of the investigation. Most of the other detectives had gone home for the night, and it was quiet, the only noise the annoying hum of the fluorescent lights.

Anna lifted the lid on a steaming container of spicy pork. Passing him a plate, napkin, and chopsticks, she said, "You are a sweet man. Did anybody ever tell you that?"

Cullen snickered. "You'd say that to anybody who brought you food."

She smiled. "I suppose that's true."

They ate in silence for a few minutes. From down the hallway came the sound of a vacuum, which meant the cleaners were on their nightly round.

Anna got up, put the garbage can from their office in the hallway, and then shut the door. Back at her desk, she said,

"Did we get the final autopsy report on Lisa Bosko?"

Nodding, Cullen waited until he was finished chewing. "It says Bosko died of a single heavy blow to the back of the head. There was a circular hole in the skull a couple of inches big. She would have died instantly and there were no other injuries."

Anna took a sip of water. "If she was hit over the back of the head it suggests she was facing away from her killer. Maybe she'd turned her back or was walking away."

"Otherwise she would likely have seen him coming. But she didn't seem to have any warning, because they couldn't find defensive wounds on her hands or arms." He spooned more rice and ginger beef onto his plate. "Maybe it was spur of the moment."

"That's quite possible. It had to have been somebody she knew, someone who was with her, because if somebody came upon her, she would have heard and turned around."

He said, "Like the husband."

"That would fit. But he's got an alibi and we can't find a shred of evidence that he had anything to do with it. We've interviewed everybody who knew him. If it was the husband, you'd think we would have found something. Maybe not hard evidence, but something pointing to him."

He said, "No sign of a weapon at the farm?"

She pushed her plate away, wiped her fingers, and then picked up and read from the police report. "A team combed the area pretty thoroughly and didn't find anything obvious. The pathologist suggested the weapon might have been a hammer, something of that size. Is it possible she wasn't killed there?"

"It's possible, but there's nothing to suggest she wasn't." He consulted the report again. "She was likely dressed because they found some remnants of yellow fabric"—he looked at the pictures in the report—"with what looks like a little flower print. No other DNA found from anybody else, which isn't unusual considering the amount of time that's passed."

Anna said, "Not a hell of a lot to go with. We don't have a motive. Nobody saw her being picked up. We have a note, which seems to be our best clue, but it only tells us she was going away for a couple of days. If she did write it."

He rubbed his face. "There is the affair. Her husband says she admitted to him she'd an affair. She also told her friend."

"But who was she having it with? It seems to have been the best kept secret in town."

Cullen thought of Marlee, who'd been seeing Mike Banson, the cop, behind his back. He hadn't suspected anything. "Maybe it's not so unusual," he said, grimacing.

Marlee had called the night before, late, just as he was falling asleep. She'd had an argument with Banson and was crying, wanted to meet up. He scratched his cheek, aware of a tightness in his chest. Odd how his feelings for her had done a complete one-eighty. The only woman he could think about was Nicole Bosko. The fire in those big eyes, her soft mouth, that beautiful body. Picturing her, a warmth spread through him.

The cleaners were in the office next door. The vacuum cleaner whined through the thin walls. Cullen put the empty takeout containers back in the paper bag, then tossed it in the garbage outside their door.

When he came back, Anna said, "Maybe Lisa Bosko didn't want to keep the affair secret any longer. Could be she was killed because she wanted to tell."

"We have to find out who it was." He tapped his fingers on the desk. "Nicole Bosko doesn't seem to know. She probably never did."

Anna took a drink from a can of soda. "On the other hand, what if Nicole Bosko knew who the caller was and told her father? She wouldn't want to admit to us she'd spilled the beans, would she? Because it would mean she got her own mother killed."

"I don't think so. Besides, like you said, the husband had an iron-clad alibi and we haven't been able to find any evidence that he hired anyone."

She shrugged. "Maybe the guy who killed her was the man she'd had an affair with, and he thought Nicole knew who he was."

"It's possible, but I don't think so. Why not kill Nicole back then, too? No, I don't think she has any idea who the guy was. If she did, she'd be motivated to tell us. She really wants to know who killed her mother."

Anna nodded. "Have we talked to all of Lisa Bosko's friends?"

He counted off on his fingers. "We've spoken to four of them. The one friend knew; the others say they didn't. We could ask them again."

"I don't think we're going to get a different answer." She finished the soda, set the can on the desk. "Oh yeah, I got a call from Corcoran, the prison in California. The guy who was suspected in the other murder, the one in prison for killing two people in the drugstore, he was working on an oil rig six miles off the coast of Nigeria when Lisa Bosko went missing."

Cullen threw a pen down. "He didn't sound like our guy anyway. It was his ex-girlfriend and she was shot."

"It doesn't look like we're dealing with a serial killer. What do we tell the chief?"

"If we don't cough up something soon, we'll have to pack this case in. She's already been pulling you away every chance she gets. We'll have to stall."

Nausea roiled in Cullen's gut and he pounded his fist on the desk. They had to find out who murdered Lisa Bosko. Somebody had to pay for that. Plus, whenever he looked at her daughter, he saw the mother. And something told him Nicole wouldn't be safe until the killer was behind bars.

Anna said, "What about where she was found? The abandoned farm? It's kind of off the beaten track, and a long way from home for Lisa Bosko. You'd almost have to know it was there. Do we know who owns it?"

He consulted a file. "A developer in New Hampshire. They bought it a year ago in August from a company called First Marshall Corporation."

"Who's behind First Marshall?"

"Still trying to find out."

Anna wiped the desk with a napkin. "So how did Lisa Bosko find out about it? She went there before with her daughter, but she must have gone before. How did she know about it? It's a couple hours' drive. Surely there are abandoned places a bit closer to take pictures of."

He pinched his temples. "And why would the person who murdered her—let's say it's the same guy who picked her up from her house—bring her there?"

"Or woman. It could have been a woman. Maybe the woman was married to the guy she was having an affair with."

He nodded, sitting forward. "We should talk to her friends again, see if any of them knew about this place."

"Her husband says he didn't."

"If we can believe him."

"There's another thing," he said. "Allan Spidell."

"*The* Allan Spidell? The one who used to do those tacky television commercials in his grocery store? Oh wait, you didn't grow up around here. You couldn't have missed them if you had. What about him?"

He said, "He was at the Bosko memorial. Apparently, he was a friend of Lisa Bosko's from way back when and she worked for him for a few years as a bookkeeper. We should pay him a visit. I called him this morning but I haven't heard back from him yet."

Anna said, "That would be interesting. Word around town is he's got financial troubles. He's sunk a lot of money into his horse farm."

"What about the grocery stores?"

"They've taken a hit, apparently. Competition from bigger chain stores. Anyway, that doesn't have anything to do with Lisa Bosko's murder. But he's a piece of work. I think he's on his third wife. My sister's kid went out for a while with his son. Another piece of work. Claire, my sister, she did everything she could to put an end to it. He was seven years older than her daughter."

"Nicole Bosko went out with Jason Spidell, too, although I think they were about the same age. They got in trouble together."

"Oh, yeah. That was a big scandal at the time, her father being a big-shot doctor and all. I get the feeling she's still trying to live it down."

* * *

"What exactly do you remember?"

The question came over the phone from Emily, who called Monday evening to check up on Nicky. They'd discussed wedding preparations and had moved on to the topic of childhood memories.

"Some of the things I remember aren't clear. They're just little snippets, like my mother singing to me. This is pretty random, but I think she was a Diana Ross fan. I remember her singing "Where Did Our Love Go." And I remember the first day of school. I wanted to dress up as a bride and she let me. She took a picture of me climbing up the steps of the bus wearing this huge veil and a white dress. My dad was mortified but my mom didn't care."

Emily laughed. "I'd love to see the picture. My mother made me wear this blue plaid dress I absolutely hated. She drove me to school and spent the whole day at the back of the classroom."

"I can just see the scowl on your face." Nicky placed a sofa cushion on her lap and crossed her arms over it. "My mom was pretty easygoing. One time we were in a field. She must have been taking pictures or something. Anyway, the grass was tall and I can remember it scratched my arms. Somehow I got mud all over my shoes. I thought she would be angry but she just laughed."

"It's great you're remembering these things. They sound like good memories."

Nicky curled a lock of hair around her index finger. "One of them wasn't so good." She hesitated. "I'm not even sure it happened, or if it's something I imagined. But it's pretty vivid. I think I almost drowned."

"What happened?"

"I was in the lake at our house and I must have fallen off the dock."

"Was this before your mother died?"

"She saved me. I remember being in the water, way over my head, and looking up. I must have been on the bottom and I remember seeing somebody on the dock looking down." A suffocating feeling tightened her throat at the memory.

"Who?"

"Probably my mother. I think she jumped in and pulled me out of the water. I remember being with her on the grass after, throwing up water. I must have swallowed quite a bit of it."

Alarm tinged Emily's tone. "Was anybody else there?"

"I don't think so. Mom was crying. I don't think I'd ever seen her upset like that before. I get the feeling maybe she felt responsible, like maybe she wasn't watching me closely enough. I don't remember much else. I don't remember falling in. It must have been summertime, because I had a bathing suit on." She swallowed, recovering. "The funny thing is I phoned my dad this morning to ask about it and he'd never heard anything about it."

"Maybe your mom didn't tell him."

She walked to the window, looked out. "You're probably right. And anyway, I'm not even sure it happened. I did have a pretty vivid imagination."

Emily said, "Are the cops getting any closer to finding out who killed your mom?"

"I don't think so, at least not from what they're telling me. Whoever did this may end up getting away with it."

"They haven't given up, have they?"

"No, but there's not a lot to work with. I just wish I could remember more. I feel like I'm letting my dad down."

"I'm sure he doesn't see it that way. How's Karina doing?"

"I haven't seen her since the memorial, but I think she's okay. Karina will persevere."

She laughed. "That's pretty well her motto."

"She did a lovely job at the memorial service. I'm just not sure her heart was in it. She told me once she hated the piano."

Emily sounded surprised. "But she's so good at it."

"I know, but I remember her saying a few years back that she had to practice for hours on end and she got to a point where she dreaded it."

"How sad. What about you? Didn't you have to play?"

She chuckled. "I refused to practice more than ten minutes at a time. It drove my dad crazy but eventually he let me quit."

"Your sister should have refused."

"She never could refuse dad. I always felt like the odd person out in our little trio, but it had its benefits, too. His expectations of Karina were so high. Whereas, me, I basically did what I wanted to do."

Emily said, "That means everything you've achieved, you've done it on your own."

They talked for a few more minutes, then Emily said, "Does Karina have a boyfriend?"

"No. She hasn't outdone me in the boyfriend department. There was somebody serious, but it didn't pan out. He was an accountant and he played tenor sax in a jazz band. She seemed to like him a lot but she didn't want to talk about what went wrong."

After the call with Emily, Nicky was heating up a bowl of leftover soup when her cell phone rang again. This time it was Karina, who was at their father's house and wanted her to come out for supper.

"I've already got something planned. Can I take a rain check? Tomorrow night?"

"I'm working a twelve-hour shift tomorrow, so it won't work. I'll just tell Dad you have other plans."

Nicky sighed. "All right. I can come." A night alone would have been preferable, but she had to make an effort.

Ten minutes later, she walked out to her car in the parking lot behind her building. It was raining again—the radio had warned of flooding in some areas—and the sky was dark and gloomy. The overgrown branches of a dogwood shrub rhythmically tapped against the car. Pulling up the hood on her jacket, she slipped her key in the lock. Maybe someday she'd be able to afford a car with an automatic opener.

Something touched her arm and she jumped, then spun around, terror shooting through her.

When she saw who it was, she let out a big breath and put her hand over her heart. "God, Mike, you scared the shit out of me."

His answer was a mumble. "Didn't mean to."

Rummaging in her purse, Nicky found her wallet and pulled out a ten-dollar bill. Mike was a homeless man she'd first seen a month ago when he started hanging out on the street near her apartment. About her age, he was unfailingly polite, didn't drink as far as she knew and was getting help for mental health issues. At least she hoped he was. He'd been on the street since February, when his mother died.

She handed him the money. "How's the job hunt going?"

Thanking her for the money with a nod, Mike flipped his hand back and forth in a gesture meaning so-so, then walked away.

The road was slick with rain and she drove slowly, still jumpy. It didn't help she'd been feeling paranoid, a strange sixth sense telling her the killer was watching.

You're being ridiculous.

Shivering, she reached over and turned on the radio. Amy Winehouse was singing about waking up alone. She switched it off.

Outside of town, the tires hissed on the wet pavement, a silvery blue ribbon in the fading light. Up ahead, on the other side of the road, a dog that looked like a German shepherd trotted down the road toward her. She slowed and when she got closer realized it was a coyote. It had gray and brown fur and pointed ears. She'd seen them in this area before, and this one looked healthy and strong. It glanced at her car with mild interest, then continued on its way.

She turned off the main road and onto the back road to her father's house. For the first section, the road was lined with tall fir trees and it was like driving through a dark tunnel. Then it opened up and she had to slow down as it wound its way above the shimmering lake. No other cars were in sight and for no reason a feeling of paranoia returned, making her stomach nauseated. Coming out had been a bad idea. She should have stayed at home and gone to bed early. It didn't help that the car felt wobbly. Her thumping heart kept time to the steady beat of the windshield wipers.

Trying to distract herself, she thought of Cullen Fraser, and those blue eyes, the way he had looked at her when they'd been in the kitchen of the old farmhouse. Instantly, a warmth flooded every part of her body.

Suddenly, a noise, loud and booming like a shotgun blast, reverberated through the car. In the next instant, a whooshing sound filled the stillness of the night, and then the deflated tire hit the road.

Screaming, she gripped the wheel and tried to keep the car straight as the steel rim ground against the pavement, sending sparks flying. Pulse racing and her whole body trembling, she fought a losing battle to keep the car on the road. Out of the corner of her eye, she saw a tire shoot out across the pavement and bounce over the short guard rail and down the steep bank to the lake.

As her car pulled to the left, her headlights bounced off the guardrail. A second or two later, she smashed into the tin barrier and the car flew through the air.

CHAPTER THIRTEEN

The car shot straight into the dusky gray sky. Everything seemed to slow down, as if Nicky were in some weird time warp. As she gripped the steering wheel, jumbled thoughts raced through her mind.

Dad warned you to take the car in for maintenance.

You're never going to get out of this alive.

It's your own stupid fault.

Then the car hit the water, front end first. Her head snapped forward, then back, as her body jolted against the seat belt. The impact broke the windshield, and a torrent of icy water gushed into the car as it plowed deep into the lake, instantly immersing her. The water tumbled about like in a washing machine.

Squeezing her mouth shut, water rushed up her nostrils and she clamped a hand over her nose to plug it. The car sank farther, still pitched at an angle, an eerie glow coming from the headlights.

She spun her head around, checked all directions. The dark, murky water made it impossible to see beyond a few feet. She had to get out.

Her hands were cold and she couldn't find the clasp to undo the seat belt. Her lungs demanded air. The car hit bottom with a little bounce, and the rear end came down. She tried the buckle again and it opened. Next the door, but it wouldn't budge. Her chest burning and ears hissing, panic set in. The door was supposed to open. Something about equalized pressure.

You're going to drown.

She groped for the lever to lower the window, but couldn't feel it. Her hair floated in the murky water like seaweed, making it even harder to see. Empty lungs screamed for air.

Squeezing her mouth shut, she fought burgeoning panic. Looked ahead to the large, jagged hole in the front windshield. She would have to go out there. Maneuvering out of her seat, she used her arms to clear safety glass out of the way, then crawled through the opening and out of the car.

Which way was up?

She kicked mindlessly, her jeans like heavy weights on her legs. Her head was about to burst.

It was just like the time at the lake all those years ago. Except her mother couldn't save her now.

She kicked harder. Bubbles rose around her head.

She kicked, clawed at the water with her hands. And then her head broke the surface. She gasped, gulping in air, flailing her arms above the small waves. She had no strength left. It didn't help that she'd never been a strong swimmer. Seaweed tangled in her arms, its strands like the tentacles of a vicious animal trying to drag her under.

In the moonlight, the shoreline was barely visible about a hundred yards away, maybe more. Above it was the road. She darted her eyes around. Couldn't see any cars, anybody. She was all alone, the darkness like a blanket smothering her. She forced her arms to swim in a messy front crawl, using all her strength, sticking her head above the waves every one or two strokes to gulp air.

You can do this.

Soon her hips sunk with every breath, so she switched to a side kick. She swallowed water, gagged. Her arms were seizing up in the icy water. Her lungs burned.

She couldn't give up. Each kick was a battle for her life.

When she couldn't go farther, she stopped to tread water. He toes touched something soft and muddy. The bottom.

She swam more, forced herself to do five strokes. Another five.

When she could stand, she waded through the water until it was at her waist, then staggered up to the shore and collapsed.

* * *

His cell phone woke Cullen out of a deep sleep. It was classical music, usually soothing, but not at five in the morning. When the cop on the other end told him Nicole Bosko's car had gone into a lake, he bolted upright.

The cop said, "I knew she was involved in your cold case, so I decided to give you a call."

Panic filled him. "How is she?"

"She's okay. They're keeping her in hospital overnight but she's all right."

"What happened?"

"She said a tire came off and she went over the guardrail. She says she wasn't going fast, but we haven't been able to determine speed yet."

Cullen put the phone on speaker and pulled on a pair of jeans. "Where'd this happen?"

"On the road near her father's place. She was going up there to see him."

Shit.

"Are we sure somebody didn't do something to her car?"

"No reason to think so, but we'll have to haul the car out of the water to get a better look. A woman who lived just up the road noticed the smashed guardrail and stopped her car to check. Lucky she did. She found Bosko on the shoreline."

Putting on a T-shirt, he said, "Any other cars around?"

"Bosko didn't see any others and the woman who called for help didn't, either. So far, nobody else has come forward."

Cullen didn't say anything, but already he had his own suspicions. Somebody might have done something to Nicole's car. Thanking the cop, he asked to be kept updated.

Off the phone, he ran downstairs and grabbed his car keys. Fear had his stomach in a vise. Somebody had tried to kill Nicole, he was sure of it.

Outside, it was still dark. At this hour, there was barely any traffic and he rushed through the quiet, gloomy streets, arriving at the hospital fifteen minutes later.

The charge nurse on the unit that had admitted Nicole took a good look at his badge, then told him Nicole was all right, aside from mild hypothermia and superficial cuts and bruises. They were keeping her overnight for observation.

The door to her room was ajar. She was sleeping. It was a private room, dark except for a dim light above her bed and some light coming through the window of her door. He stood beside her, reached over, and smoothed hair away from her forehead. She looked pale and fragile, like a kid.

He couldn't leave her here alone. She wasn't safe, wouldn't be until he found out who had killed her mother, and now tried to kill her. Pulling up a chair, he sat down, tried to figure out what he would do next. He had to talk to her, try to find out what happened, but didn't want to wake her up.

Just before eight a.m., a nurse in pink scrubs came in. She nodded at him, then went to the other side of the bed, wrapped a blood pressure cuff around Nicole's arm, and started a machine to get the pressure.

Opening her eyes, Nicole blinked for a minute, uncomprehending, and she glanced around. Spotting him, her eyes widened, as if she were surprised to see him.

The nurse left and he pulled the chair closer. Her hair was all messed up and smelled like lake water and seaweed. He wanted to stroke her pale face and hold her hand, but settled with words. "How are you feeling?"

"I'm all right." Her answer was a hoarse whisper.

"Do your father and sister know what happened?"

"The hospital called them last night and I saw them for a few minutes just after midnight. I talked to my sister on the phone this morning. They're coming back in in a few hours."

He nodded. "Tell me what happened."

She rubbed her temples. "Can you help me put this bed up?"

Finding a control panel on the side, he raised the front of the bed so she could sit up. He sat back down.

She thanked him. "There's not much to tell. I was driving to my father's house and something went wrong with the car. I think one of the tires was loose, the front one. I saw it go across the road and over the guardrail. I tried to keep the car on the road, but I couldn't." Her eyes were wet.

Swallowing a hard lump in his throat, he said, "It's okay. You're all right now."

Her lips trembled and her eyes were as big as saucers. She looked more scared than he'd ever seen her. Her left arm was hooked up to an intravenous line. He focused on the pole for a moment, tried to swallow that lump wedged in his throat.

Her hand clutched a bunched up section of thin white blanket. "The car went right through the guardrail. When I hit the water, it filled up right away. I couldn't believe how fast it happened. And it was so cold. I had a hard time getting out." Tears rolling down her cheeks, she grabbed a tissue and wiped her eyes.

Grinding his teeth, Cullen jumped up, paced to the window. "Did you see any other cars?"

"I didn't see anybody. The first person was the woman who found me on the shore. Can you find out her name? I'd like to thank her."

"Sure, sure." He sat down again. "But how did it happen?

Tires don't just come off. Have you had it serviced lately?"

"What's lately?"

"Jesus, Nicole."

Lowering her brow, she squinted at him. "Don't get mad at me. I feel stupid enough already."

"I'm sorry. I shouldn't have said that. We don't know that it's your fault." He didn't want to say he suspected it wasn't, that somebody had tried to kill her by sabotaging her car.

She reached for the call bell hooked to the front of her bed. "I'm going to call the nurse to see how soon I can get out of here."

Reaching over, he snatched it out of her hand. "Wait, wait. What's the hurry?" He'd get a guard on the door and she'd be safer here than out of the hospital.

"I'm fine. What? Why are you looking at me like that?"

Maybe a little bit of fear would be a good thing. What right did he have to not reveal his suspicions? "What if somebody did something to your car?"

"You just said it was my fault for not getting the car serviced."

"I did not."

Her eyes narrowed. "You certainly implied it."

He massaged his forehead with one hand, then looked up to meet her eyes. "Maybe someone loosened the nuts that were used to keep the tire on. Until we learn more, we have to be extra careful."

Her mouth dropped open. "Why would somebody want to hurt me? I don't even know anything. Believe me, if I thought I did, I'd tell you. But there's nothing."

"What did you do yesterday?"

"I went to work, and then afterward I went home, talked to Emily on the phone. It was an uneventful day."

He scratched his head. "And the day before? Sunday?"

She thought about it a minute, hesitated. "Well, I went to see Allan Spidell."

Alarmed, he jumped to his feet. "What? Why the hell did you do that?"

She drew back, bit her lip. "It was no big deal. I just wanted to talk to him about my mom."

"What did he tell you?"

"I asked him if he'd had an affair with my mother. He said no, but he didn't like the suggestion. I was hoping he'd be able to give me more information, but I don't think he's hiding anything. And I don't think he would try to kill me just for asking questions. It doesn't make sense."

"Nothing about this makes sense. Why didn't you let me go see him? You don't go off all half-cocked—"

She sat up straighter, shook her head. "I told you about it, but you didn't seem too interested."

He clenched his fists. "What are you talking about? I was interested and I did plan to see him."

Her eyes on him were dark and determined. "This has nothing to do with Allan Spidell. What reason would he have to hurt me? I don't have some secret knowledge about him that would threaten him."

Irritation quickened his pulse. "Let me be the judge of that. You have no idea what he's capable of."

She looked at him closely. "What do you mean?"

"He may be involved in stuff that's not exactly on the up and up."

"Like what?"

"He's got big money problems. He seems to be embroiled in some kind of dispute with his business partners."

"What could his money problems possibly have to do with me?"

"Maybe nothing. Maybe he just doesn't want police attention. Maybe your mother found out something all those years ago."

She blew out a noisy breath. "She did bookkeeping work for him. If she'd found out something bad, she would have gone to the police. She would have told my father." Her tone was dismissive.

"Listen, we don't know anything for sure yet. And I don't want you putting your life in danger."

She pursed his lips. "I admit he did make me feel a little uncomfortable. Allan Spidell's got a big temper."

"What did he say to you?"

"He asked me to leave. I doubt I'll be going there again."

"I'll go see him." He stroked his chin. "Do you park your car in the lot behind your apartment building?" When she nodded, he said, "So anybody could have access to your car? Did you leave it unattended yesterday?"

Shivering again, she nodded. "I walked to work."

"Does your building have surveillance cameras?"

She shook her head no.

"Your car is being pulled out of the lake this morning. I should get at least a preliminary report on it within a couple of days."

She paled. "You're scaring me."

"Maybe that's not such a bad thing. We've got to figure out a way to keep you safe until this is all over."

She closed her eyes. "I'm not staying here."

He nodded. The hospital wasn't safe, either, now that he thought about it. Getting her somewhere safer had to be a priority.

She said, "I'm not going to stay with my father or my sister. Don't even suggest it. They've got enough on their plates. I'll figure something out."

"What about a friend?"

"I don't want to put a friend at risk. No way." She scoffed. "I'll find a hotel. My friend Emily's mother owns a hotel."

The idea wasn't appealing. A hotel wasn't safe enough. Unless it was in Alaska.

She pinched her lips. "This is so crazy. I know nothing."

"Maybe you do. You just don't realize it yet." Rubbing his neck, he said, "A hotel won't do; it's too risky. I'll find somewhere safe for you to stay."

She crossed her arms. "No way am I putting this on my father or sister."

"Don't worry." Heck, he had an extra room at his place. If he stashed her there and kept her hidden, nobody would be the wiser. He turned to her. "I'll come up with something."

"I am not your responsibility." Her chin was up but it wasn't hard to see the fear in her eyes. He wanted to reassure her, but he also wanted her scared. It would help keep her alive.

"I'm having a cop put on the door until you're discharged.

Then I'll pick you up. We can stop by your place and pick up some clothes."

* * *

"You look a bit better now than last night," Karina said as she and James Bosko approached Nicky's bedside at Riverton General Hospital. "We were so worried. You looked awful."

Nicky propped pillows behind her back so she could sit up. "I'm feeling fine, honestly. It's all over now. There's no reason to worry."

It was just after ten a.m. She'd dozed off after Cullen left. The nurse had closed her door and the quiet din of the hospital was almost hypnotic.

Karina clutched her hand tightly and kissed her on the cheek. "Worried doesn't begin to describe it." Stepping back, she held up a bouquet of colorful flowers, then left the room in search of a vase, promising to be right back. Her father sat down on the bed, leaned over, and kissed her. Unshaven, his clothes were rumpled, as if he had slept in them. "We wondered why you didn't come. We tried your cell phone. We waited a long time."

Nicky reached a hand out to him, tried to smile. "I'm fine. I should be out of here, but for some reason they kept me in overnight. As soon as the doctor comes by, I'll get the okay to go home."

Sharp eyes studied her. "What happened?"

She forced a shrug. "I should have had the car in for maintenance. One of the tires came off." A barrage of images hit her, making her heart race. Hitting the guardrail, tearing through the sky, water flooding the car. Desperately trying to open the car door, her lungs bursting from lack of air.

Her father patted her hand. "You're okay now. I'll make sure you're safe."

She took a deep breath, then another, tried to slow her heart rate. "I was so scared," she managed to choke out. "I've never been so scared in my life."

Tears gathered in her father's eyes. "It would break my heart if anything happened to you."

Nicky cleared her throat. "Nothing's going to happen." Her father was stressed enough about everything as it was. Adding to it would be cruel—even dangerous, considering his heart attack. She remembered visiting him in the hospital a year ago. He'd looked so gray and tired. Much as he looked like now. The doctor had said the first heart attack put him at greater risk of having a second. The realization hit like a punch to the stomach. She had to protect him at all costs.

Karina came back in, set the flowers on the windowsill. She pulled up a chair and sat next the bed.

"What did the police say? Are they treating this seriously?" Her father's trembling hands held hers and when she didn't respond right away, he said, "Don't you dare hold back on your dad." A flash of irritation darkened his eyes, anger eclipsing worry at least for a moment.

Nicky bit her lip. "They have to take a look at the car before they can say anything. But they did suggest I might have been going too fast." An outright lie, that was. Another one followed. "They said cars often go off the road in that spot and speeding's almost always to blame."

This seemed to placate him. "You have to be more careful, Nicole."

Karina shook her head slowly at her sister, her expression managing to convey both a mild reprimand and total lack of surprise. They talked for a few more minutes, and then Karina sent their father down to the cafeteria for coffee.

When he had gone, Karina pulled her chair closer. "What is going on, Nicky? What are you not telling us?"

Nicky took Karina's shaking hand in hers. "What can I say, I've got a lead foot."

Karina's brow furrowed, but she let it go. She was a detail person, and she asked pointed questions about what had happened when the car went in the water. Nicky gave her a shortened version, making it sound like her escape had been a piece of cake.

"You have to be more careful, Nicole."

Nicky bit her lip. Karina and her father seemed to have no trouble believing Nicky was responsible for what had happened. She half-believed it herself. But maybe Cullen's suspicions weren't so far-fetched. It was possible somebody had tried to kill her. An icy coldness gripped her, made her shiver.

What if the same person who'd killed her mother was coming after her? She was the one who supposedly knew something. Even though she didn't, the killer might think she did. He or she didn't want to risk keeping her alive.

Karina said, "Promise to be more careful?"

Nicky managed a nod. With her father returning at any

moment, the high road seemed the best choice. Still, what if she was all wrong, and her sister and father were in danger, too? She grabbed Karina's hand. "It's probably a good idea to have your cars checked, just to be on the safe side." They both parked their cars in garages, but people might still be able to get at them when they parked elsewhere, like at the hospital.

Karina darkened. "What?"

She tried to placate her. "Don't we all go to the same mechanic? What if they were careless about the tires?"

Karina narrowed her eyes. "Come stay with me in town, or the three of us could stay together at the lake. It'd feel better."

And put them in danger? No way. "I'm not sure when they'll let me go." She changed the subject before Karina could object. "Is Dad going to be okay?"

"He's holding it together, but just barely. He wanted to go back to work, but he can't. He's having trouble sleeping. He should probably see a doctor but he won't hear anything of it. He keeps looking at photographs of Mom."

"What about you? How are you feeling?" Her sister spent so much time worrying about her father that sometimes Nicky wondered if she had anything left for herself.

"I'm fine. I'll be okay."

But a strange sort of light in her eyes, like panic, put the statement in doubt. It was almost as if she knew Nicky hadn't been responsible for the crash. Squeezing Karina's hand, she didn't know what to say to comfort her sister that wouldn't be a lie and she'd already lied enough today. So she didn't say anything.

CHAPTER FOURTEEN

That afternoon, Cullen loaded Nicky's small suitcase and three boxes of photos into the trunk of his car and helped her into the passenger seat.

He said, "Did you pack enough clothes?" Her suitcase looked not much bigger than Marlee's makeup case.

"It's not more than a couple of days, right? I called them at the shelter this morning and told them I'd be back to work in a couple of days."

"Let's hope so." He put the car in gear and pulled out of the parking lot of her apartment building.

She tapped her foot on the floor on the car. She hadn't said much since they'd left the hospital. Fear seemed a reasonable explanation but he figured she was more upset she'd let him talk her into finding a place for her to lay low.

Just wait until she found out it was his place.

They stopped at a store for a prepaid cell phone, then hit the main road east out of town. Half an hour later, after another five miles on a gravel country road, he drove the car up his long lane and stopped at the side of his one-and-a-half-story farmhouse.

He opened the car door and got out. "You coming?"

Still sitting, she looked around. "Whose place is this?"

He dipped his head down and looked inside the car at her. "Mine."

"Yours?" She crossed her arms, glared at him. "Why didn't you tell me? I can't stay here."

Getting back in the car, he sat down, leaving the door open. "Why not?"

"I can think of a dozen good reasons." She shook her head in disbelief. "Did you tell your boss?"

"No."

"I knew it. It's against the rules, isn't it? You'll get in trouble."

"Not if we keep it quiet." The idea had occurred to him, but at this point he didn't give a shit.

"Why are you doing this?" Rubbing the back of her neck, staring straight ahead, she looked like she had no idea what the answer was.

"Because I want you to be safe." Telling her more, such as that she was becoming to mean a lot of him, didn't seem like a good idea. "It'll just be for one night. Tomorrow we'll find you somewhere else." A flat-out lie, since no other place came to mind.

She looked at him with those intense brown eyes, thought about it for a moment, then sighed deeply. "One night." She held up her index finger to reinforce the point.

Smiling to himself, he got out of the car. As he opened the trunk, she got out of the car, stood with her hands on her hips.

He said, "Sorry about the manure smell. You get that when you live out here. I don't mind it—it never gets really strong—but some people do." Marlee, for one, hated it.

From her, a chuckle. "It's fine. I lived near a farm one summer a couple of years back. I think I actually like it. Not pig, but cow's okay."

"A woman after my heart." Clutching his chest in mock delight, he grabbed the suitcase and walked to the back door. He opened the deadlock, then stepped aside to let her enter.

Walking into the old kitchen, she glanced at a miter saw mounted on a table in the corner. "Well, this is a surprise." At his raised eyebrows, she added, "I didn't have you pegged as a handyman type of guy."

"I hope that's a good thing. I haven't done much lately. The first thing would have been a new kitchen."

"You're not going to?"

He ran a hand through his hair. The house had been a sticking point with Marlee; she hated it, too. But now that they had broken up, maybe he would stay. He just hadn't had time to give it much thought. "I'm still deciding what to do. What it is I want, you know?"

She nodded. "Why not restore it? I mean, you want something functional, but I think you should try to keep some of the old character."

"Definitely. I'd like to preserve as much as I can. Start with a new kitchen and bathroom. It's just taking a bit longer than I expected to figure it all out." He took a breath. Stop rambling.

What did it matter what she thought of the place? "Anyway, I'll show you where you'll be sleeping."

She walked down the hallway into the small living room, took in the old light fixture on the ceiling, the mullioned windows and wood floors. "I love the floors."

"Pine, milled by hand. They're pretty rustic, with all the knots and holes, but I like them."

She nodded. "How old is it?"

"A hundred and forty-nine years. My great-great-great-grandfather on my mother's side built it, but it was sold out of the family when my grandfather died." He set down the suitcase. "Two years ago it came up for sale and I snapped it up. I couldn't resist. I think it's Greek or Gothic revival."

"One of those revivals." A smile curved her lips, transforming her face into the most beautiful he'd ever seen. His heart skipped a couple of beats.

He gestured to an old leather sofa and a tub chair. "As you can see, I don't have much furniture. Sorry."

"Stop apologizing. It's lovely." She pointed to the sofa. "I can sleep there."

"I have an inflatable bed tucked away somewhere. It will be more comfortable. Or you can have my bed." Even though the house was safe, he didn't want her sleeping downstairs if he was upstairs.

"No, not your bed." She flushed. "I realize you didn't mean it that way. I just don't want to make any trouble."

"It's no trouble."

"For somebody who doesn't like trouble and stress, unfortunately, I'm a bit inclined to cause it."

"Stop it. It's no trouble. What's today? Tuesday? I'm off until Thursday." He smiled. "I'll go get the photos from the car."

He brought in the boxes and bags in two trips and left them on the living room floor. Nicole's suitcase was gone from the hallway and he could hear her upstairs.

In the kitchen, he made coffee and brought two mugs and a plate of biscuits. When he returned to the living room, Nicole was sitting on the sofa, leaning forward, and looking down at an open photo album on her lap. A strand of dark hair fell across her face and she brushed it back, exposing a long and elegant neck. A couple of buttons of her shirt were undone, providing a glimpse of the tops of her breasts spilling out of a lacy white bra.

A fierce desire gripped him, making every nerve in his body tingle. The urge to touch her, and be touched by her, was agony. Heat flooded his body.

He walked into the kitchen, poured himself a glass of water. *She's here so you can keep her safe. That's it.*

He just hadn't considered how much of a temptation being around her all the time would be.

* * *

An hour later, Nicky looked through the tall living room windows across the fields surrounding the house. On both sides of the house were unobstructed views of the gently rolling landscape. Her friend Emily, who had some claustrophobia, had once said her dream landscape was open farmland and Nicky could see why. Watching the dairy cattle dawdling in the pasture field, she let herself pretend for a moment all was right with the world.

Reality came crashing back when Cullen returned with an armload of split wood, which he dumped in a box beside the fireplace in the living room.

It wasn't just herself who was in danger. Now Cullen was, too. A tight band wrapped her chest. Why had she let him talk her into this?

She sat on the sofa while he crumpled up some newspaper. "I'll just light a little fire, just enough to take the chill off."

Nodding, she looked down, held her eyes open wide to try to stop crying. If she started, it was game over.

Little flames licked at the logs in the grate. Brushing dirt off his hands, Cullen turned around. "I'm just going to throw together some sandwiches. Is tuna on rye all right? Beer?"

"That'd be great. You want help?"

He shook his head. "Just relax."

A few minutes later, he set the sandwiches and two bottles of beer on the table, then sat down beside her.

She pointed to a picture she'd found in the oldest album. "That's my mother's mother, my grandmother. Apparently she left her husband when my mom was little. She took my mom with her."

Cullen leaned over to look at it. "Any idea why?"

"My Uncle Steve told me once my grandfather was abusive. I'm not sure how he knew, since it was the other side of the family." She shrugged. "I haven't seen many pictures of him. I had the feeling from what my uncle said my mother didn't remember much of him."

"Is he still alive?"

She took a bite of the sandwich, washed it down with a swig of beer. "He died about ten years ago. My sister found his obituary online and showed it to me."

Another photo showed her mother standing in the side yard of their house at the lake, leaning against a four-foot-high cedar fence, one arm stretched along the top. She was wearing a dress, white or cream with a print of tiny flowers. It was what they would call a shirtdress, short sleeved with a thin belt in the same fabric. She was looking directly at the camera, maybe ready to smile.

She said, "I remember her wearing that dress." Was it the last she saw her mother alive, or some other time?

Cullen examined the picture closely. "When was this taken?" His face had paled.

She shrugged. "No idea. Why?" The band around her chest tightened again. "Tell me."

"I'm pretty sure it was the dress she was found in," he said, not meeting her eyes. "It was partially decomposed but there was enough left to make me think this is it. It looks like the same pattern, the flowers. They were a mustardy yellow."

She sat back, looked down, and held her eyes wide to stop tears.

Cullen reached over, put his arm around her. "I'm sorry. I shouldn't have said that."

He left his arm there and stroked her forearm. More than anything else in the world, she wanted to lean against him and feel his arms around her. For comfort, nothing more, even though her feelings for him were deepening. But if she did, there would be no turning back. For all she knew, he hadn't made a final split with the girlfriend.

Sitting forward, she shifted away slightly on the sofa. She wasn't ready for this. She felt vulnerable and disconnected from what was going on, as if some sort of defense mechanism had kicked in to keep the terror at bay. It'd started when she'd learned of her mother's death and intensified after last night's crash. It was all too unreal, almost as if it wasn't her sitting here, being comforted by the man with the electric eyes, but someone else. She didn't have enough control over herself to be responsible for making good decisions.

After taking in one slow breath, then another, she reached for the photo album and looked at the picture again. "Is it significant in some way, to know what she was wearing?"

His hand shifted off her arm. "Did she wear it a lot?"

"I don't think so. I only saw it on her once, maybe twice. I think it was for special occasions. Dresses weren't her thing. She was more a jeans and T-shirt type, like me. It is odd, though, that she would wear it to a farm, don't you think?"

He pursed his lips. "I agree."

"Maybe she wasn't expecting to go to the farm." Something flickered deep in her mind, like grass in a field, but she couldn't grasp it and it was gone.

An odd look was on his face. "What is it?"

"It's frustrating. I keep thinking I remember something, but I can't grab hold of whatever it is." She shrugged. "You should ask my dad or my sister about the dress. She might have worn it more often."

From the looks of it, many of the pictures in this album

had been taken in the last year of her life, because Nicky was in some of them and looked about four or five years old. The subjects varied. Sometimes the pictures were of her sister and herself, but in other cases, her father must have taken them because the girls were with their mother. Only two pictures had the whole family. The candid photos were the best, even though in one Nicky was crying, her mouth open in midwail while Karina laughed in the background.

Cullen pointed to a picture of her father and her Uncle Steve, standing in the backyard of her father's house. "Your dad is close to his brother, isn't he?"

"Very. They always have been. My father is proud of his little brother, of what he's accomplished."

"Surely your father considers himself successful?"

"He does, but his brother was always so quiet. I get the feeling it was a bit of a surprise he did so well with his business. Maybe I'm reading more into it than is there, but from what I gather they had a hard time growing up. Their father was an autocrat, not easy to live with, very demanding. He was always pushing the boys to do better, making them compete with each other. My uncle was a football star, a running back, really fast. My father didn't make the team, although he says he didn't try very hard." She chuckled, remembering how her father and uncle had chided each other over Thanksgiving turkey one year.

She said, "I'll find you a picture of my grandfather from my father's side." She leafed through an album, found a picture near the back. He was sitting in a lawn chair, reading a paper, and looking up with a scowl at the photographer. "He was a

dentist. But he lived downstate, so I never had to go to him."
She grimaced. "Thank God for that."

"But your father was strict with you, wasn't he?"

"I suppose so, but not like his father, and you have to remember my dad was a single parent. It must have been pretty tough for him. I didn't adjust well when my mother was gone. As I got older, my sister was forced into the role of peacekeeper."

He watched her closely, those eyes intent on her, and she thought back to the first time they'd met. That he was helping her was crazy.

The way he looked at her, intense and serious, was seriously sexy. It made her feel warm and tingly all over her body.

Cullen said, "Your uncle looks a lot like your father. Do they have similar personalities as well?"

"They are a lot alike, but my Uncle Steve is quieter, more thoughtful."

"How so?"

"He does a lot of good works. He's involved in charity, but he does it quietly. He doesn't seem to want to draw attention to himself. With my father, his relief work is well known, although I suppose it's because he's always trying to raise money for the countries he goes to."

She put the album down, finished her beer. "I was hoping there was something here to help us in some way, make me remember something, but I can't find anything."

Cullen gestured to the boxes. "What about those?"

"Those are my mother's hobby photos. I've had a good look through them, but I don't see anything that stands out. Maybe fresh eyes will see something I don't."

Closing her eyes, the image of her mother in the yellow dress filled her head, and without warning, tears filled her eyes. Sadness, anger at a life cut short. The repercussions had reverberated down through the years, and would likely continue for a long time. As an empty feeling came crashing down inside her, she started to sob.

Moving closer, Cullen put his hands around her and pulled her toward him. She let herself lean against him this time, not caring. He felt warm and strong and smelled like soap.

A while later, finally able to stop crying, she turned her head, looked at him, let herself examine his face, chin, lips, forehead. Their eyes met.

He brushed her hair behind her ears. "Are you okay?"

She nodded, not trusting herself to speak. They both knew this was dangerous territory but neither of them broke eye contact until she reached out and touched a little scar above his lip, just below his moustache. "How did you get this?"

"It's actually a mild cleft lip." He took her hand and something in his expression suggested fear. Or maybe she was seeing things. "I want to ask you something."

She cleared her throat, waited. His smell, fresh and woodsy, was mesmerizing.

"Can I kiss you? Just one kiss?" Husky, his voice had gone all low and husky.

She nodded. "I won't even call you an asshole."

He wasn't in the mood for light remarks. Those blue eyes smoldered. His lips were soft and full, slightly parted, utter temptation. It was torture looking at him and not doing anything.

She put her hands around his neck, pulled him closer, and his mouth on hers was as light as a feather. His lips trailed along hers, reached the corners, went back to the middle, and then his tongue moved along the seam of her lips, slipped inside her mouth, then out.

Warmth flooded her and she shuddered, totally unprepared for her reaction. Until now, they had hardly touched and even now his hands weren't on her. It was just his tongue, soft, darting in and out. His five o'clock shadow prickled her skin.

He pulled away. Her eyes fluttered open and met his, and then she lowered her eyes. For a moment, he didn't say or do anything, then dipped his head down so he could see her eyes. "See? I kept my promise, just a kiss."

She swallowed, looked away.

He said, "We should call it a night. I'll get the inflatable bed set up."

CHAPTER FIFTEEN

The next morning, Cullen was lying in bed staring at the ceiling when his phone buzzed on the nightstand beside his bed.

"I know it's your day off, but I thought you'd want to be kept up to date," Anna Ackerman said when he answered.

He groaned. "What time is it?" It had taken hours to fall asleep and he'd tossed and turned all night, unable to stop thinking about Nicole.

"Eight thirty. Time to get up and at 'em."

Another groan. "What'd you want to tell me?"

"First Marshall Corporation belongs to Allan Spidell."

"First Marshall? What's that again?"

"The holding company that sold the farm where Lisa Bosko's body was found."

He bolted up, swung his legs over the side of the bed. "Shit."

"I'd say. It might be just the break we need. Want to head over to his place?"

"Definitely. We should ask him about that and why Lisa Bosko quit working for him just before she was killed. I'm thinking maybe they had a falling out. She found out something, and he killed her to keep her quiet."

"Why are you whispering?"

"Am I whispering?" he whispered, slipping into a pair of jeans. He walked down the hallway to the door of Nicole's bedroom, which was ajar. Peeking in, he saw crumpled sheets but no Nicole. Her suitcase was open on the floor beside the bed.

Looking around downstairs, Nicole was nowhere to be seen. A fissure of unease licked at him. In the kitchen, his keys were on the table by the window.

"You there?" Anna said with a trace of irritation.

"Call you back in a minute." He hung up before she could respond.

Back upstairs, he looked out the front window. It was narrow, with a pointed arch at the top. Didn't see her. Ran down the hallway to his bedroom, peered out a side window. Let out a breath. She was in the uncut hayfield, about a half mile off, walking back toward the house.

He called Anna back. "I'll just grab some coffee and breakfast. I can pick you up in, say, an hour. I'll call you when I'm leaving."

Nicole was knee-deep in the grass, and the tops swaying in the wind seemed to wrap around her. In a week or two, the farmer who rented the field would cut the hay. Above her the sky was a cloudless blue. He watched her for a long time, thinking of their kiss, and soon she was close enough to see she was wearing the same navy sweater from last night. The sun caught coppery highlights in her hair. She walked with her hands in her back pockets of her jeans. When she looked up and saw him at the window, she took her hands out and gave a little wave.

A feeling of warmth spread through him. Turning from the window, he put on a white button-down shirt and went downstairs to start breakfast. By the time she came in, he had coffee ready and bacon and eggs on the go. While she poured herself a coffee, he set their breakfasts on the table, retrieved cutlery and salt and pepper. "How'd you sleep?"

"Well, thank you."

It was doubtful she was telling the truth. She looked tired but better than the day before. Better and then some in a plaid shirt with the top two buttons undone. He speared a piece of bacon, tried not to think about reaching over and slipping his hand in the opening.

Stop staring.

He said, "I have to go out for a while, a couple of hours." He didn't want to tell her where until he had more information, not wanting her to think about Allan Spidell. "Will you be okay here?"

"I'll be fine. I took a peek at your bookcase. I might just find something to read."

"Help yourself to anything. There's not much food in the fridge, but enough to throw together a sandwich, in case you get hungry. The mobile's on the counter, if you want to reach me. I put my number in it."

Half an hour later, he picked up Anna downtown and headed for the Spidell ranch.

Anna had brought a file with an interview with Spidell from when Lisa Bosko had disappeared. She said, "He didn't have much to say. He gave Bosko the job as a sort of favor. They were old high school friends and she'd come to him eighteen months earlier, wanting to earn some extra cash. He said she was very good at it. He had no idea why she left, but she gave two weeks' notice."

He said, "She wouldn't just quit her job and give no explanation."

"I agree, but it might not have anything to do with this. And back then the cops had no reason to suspect Spidell, or anyone else, for that matter."

Just before Taunton Lake, driving past a new subdivision, he spotted the Spidell ranch on a hill ahead. "Did you find anything out about what his money troubles are all about?"

She nodded. "There's a dispute with one of his business partners, a Lewis Mandrake. It's hard to pin it down, but it seems things went sour in the last year or so. The partner says Spidell owes him a lot of money, somewhere between three and four million dollars. Spidell may have been siphoning off money into his horse farm. Mandrake is suing him."

Cullen whistled as the car pulled up in front of the house. "That's a lot of money."

As he got out of the car, the front door opened and a woman burst out, followed by Spidell's son. Cullen couldn't remember his name.

The woman was yelling and flapping her hands about. She tripped on the last step, caught herself.

He said, "What's going on?"

"What?" This came from the son. "We called you. We called the police."

In the distance, the noise of sirens came across the fields and up the hill. "What happened?"

The son said, "It's my father. He's killed himself. He hung himself in the barn."

* * *

After Cullen left, Nicky read a magazine for a while, then found a pair of scissors in the kitchen and used them to slice the packing tape on the last unopened box of photographs, one that she'd picked up from her father's place. Opening the box, the smell of dust and mold hit her. Sneezing, she pulled out a couple of dozen photos bound together with a thin blue elastic. She sneezed again as she set them down on the table.

The box must have been stored in the basement for a long time. Removing the elastic, she riffled through the photos. This time, sneezed three times in quick succession. She spread the photos on the table so they could air out, then went into the kitchen to make a sandwich for lunch.

Cullen called as she was cleaning up, but didn't say where he was or what he was doing, although he warned her he might not be back for a couple of hours.

Back in the living room, she peered down at some of the photos. One set was of a group of teenagers outside in someone's backyard. Her mother was there, aged about eighteen, fresh faced and beautiful, her long brown hair hanging down her back. She seemed to be staring at something, but it was impossible to say what it was. If Nicky was correct, and her mother had been eighteen, it meant she'd had fewer than a dozen years to live. She put the picture down, a dark hollowness in her stomach widening.

From the other pictures, Nicky could see four girls and three boys had been together that day and they'd passed the camera around so no one was left out. It took a moment to recognize her uncle, Steve Bosko, then a grinning Allan Spidell, who was much slimmer and had a full head of hair. She didn't recognize any of the girls, aside from her mother, or the third boy, who was shorter than the other boys, with a hawkish nose and frizzy blond hair pulled back in a ponytail. She would have to ask her uncle.

After a while, sneezing again, she put the pictures aside and went for a walk. When she came back, at just past three p.m., Cullen was standing on the back step.

He looked gorgeous, rocking a serious five o'clock shadow, and his body all muscle and brawn in a white shirt and jeans.

Her chest felt like it was swelling. When he didn't return her smile her smile, she said, "What's wrong?"

"Come inside."

"Tell me." Her pulse quickening, she reached out, grabbed his arm. A chill spread over her skin. "You've arrested Allen Spidell, haven't you?"

He took her hand, and when he looked down his eyes were troubled. "No, we haven't. Allan Spidell's dead. His body was found in his barn this morning."

CHAPTER SIXTEEN

Shrinking back, Nicole gave a little cry before clamping her hands over her mouth.

Cullen cursed himself under his breath for not breaking the news more softly. She'd gone pale again, giving her face a bleached-out look.

A gust of wind blew her hair across her face. It was cold and he reached out for her. "Come inside. I'll tell you."

In the kitchen, he waited until she was seated at the table before speaking. "Jason Spidell found his father's body in the horse barn this morning. His father wasn't answering his cell, so he went out to look for him."

"And?"

"He said he found him hanging from a beam in the horse barn."

She kept her eyes on his. "Suicide?"

"Can't say for sure until the investigation is complete but it looks like it."

Hanging her head, she rubbed her face. After a minute, she looked up. "I suppose I should go see Jason."

Something burned in Cullen's chest. He didn't think she had any feelings for Spidell, but what if he had some residual pull he could use? He'd seen the way the guy had looked at Nicole at the memorial service.

Ashamed for even thinking of that, he got up and walked to the window. To the south, a small mountain peak rose above the fields, just visible in the fading light.

She said, "Do you think this has anything to do with my mother's death? Like maybe he killed my mom and felt so guilty about it he couldn't take it anymore?"

He turned to face her. "I don't know."

"It kind of makes sense." Hope crept into her voice as she warmed to the theme. "It was okay while everybody thought she'd disappeared, but now we know it was murder—and I started questioning him about his relationship with her—it was too much to handle."

Although loath to dash her hopes, he didn't want her to have a false sense of security just because Allan Spidell was dead. "It's a possibility, but I think if he'd lived with killing her for so long, I'm not sure her body being discovered would put him over the edge."

"Did he leave a note?" She put her tightly clenched hands on the table.

He shook his head to indicate no. "He was having money problems. He was being sued and maybe the pressure of it got to be too much. His wife said he'd been despondent. She wanted him to go see a doctor but he refused."

"It just seems like too much of a coincidence."

"I agree."

They discussed it some more, but too many unanswered questions made it difficult to say anything with certainty.

After a while, he went outside and started up the barbecue and they had burgers and a salad. Later, they grabbed sweaters and he built a fire in a pit in the backyard he'd made of river rock.

She sat in a folding chair nursing a beer, not saying much. After a while, she said, "We may never find out who killed my mother or why." She met his eyes. "I'm not blaming you. I realize you're trying your best. But I don't know how I'll be able to cope with not knowing."

He said, "I haven't given up."

She didn't seem to have heard him. "The more I think about, the more I realize Allan Spidell didn't kill her. He didn't have a motive. He seemed to like her." She poked at the fire with a long stick. "In some ways he seemed protective of her, almost like a big brother."

"Even brothers and sisters can have complicated relationships. If you dig under the surface, all sorts of nuances show up."

She nodded. "Don't I know it? Except in my family, it's important to show to the outside world everything is perfect. A lot of it is smoke and mirrors, isn't it?"

Fully dark now, stars filled the sky. The back porch light cast a dim glow across the yard. Wood in the fire, some of it still a bit green, hissed and popped, but it gave off a lot of heat. Cullen took off his sweater, draped it over the arm of the chair.

The crickets that had chirped up a raucous storm a few weeks ago were dormant now.

He said, "Still, I bet you'd do anything for your sister, wouldn't you?"

She spoke without hesitation. "Of course. Ask me ten years ago and you might have gotten a different answer, and she still drives me crazy sometimes, but I do love her and I'd do anything for her."

He threw another log onto the bonfire and took a long swig of beer. "My brother and I have a pretty uncomplicated relationship."

Nicole stood up suddenly, threw the stick she'd been holding on the ground.

Startled, he said, "What?"

She was already half way to the house. "I have to look at the pictures again," she yelled over her shoulder.

He caught up with her in the living room, where she knelt on the floor and opened a box. She looked through a few pictures, then set it aside. Picking up a photo album, she flipped through it. She must have found what she was looking for, because she sat back, her bum on her heels, and started looking at them more closely.

He said, "You want to tell me what's going on?"

After examining it, she stood up and handed it to him. "What do you see?"

The light from the lamp in the corner wasn't bright, so he walked into the kitchen, flipped on the overhead light, and studied the picture. Following him, she stood to the side, waiting.

He said, "I see your mother, Allan Spidell, another girl, and your father. It looks like they're at a high school party."

She snatched the picture away, took another look.

He said, "Am I missing something?"

"That's not my father."

"It sure looks like your father."

"It's my uncle."

He frowned. "And?"

"We were talking a minute ago about relationships between sisters and brothers. How you'd do anything for them. My dad and my uncle are really close. They even look the same. That's what made me think of it."

"Made you think of what?"

"What if my uncle found out my mother was having an affair?"

He shook his head slowly. Talk about coming out of left field. "Do you have any evidence he knew? I mean, it's a bit of a leap."

"Maybe my dad confided in him. Let's just do a what-if. What do you think my uncle, who is close to my father and vice versa, would do if he found out my mother was having an affair?"

She was way off base here. "Kill her?" He shook his head, then suddenly remembered the alibi. "Wait a second. Your uncle had an alibi. He was in Connecticut with his wife."

She gave him a long look. "Alibis can be faked. What if he was motivated? Maybe if he was mad enough." Her pitch rose an octave. "He might not seem like the violent type, but in the right circumstances, who knows?"

"But are these the right circumstances? Your father said he forgave your mother. Do you honestly think he'd be helping your father by killing his wife, the woman he loved?"

A flicker of doubt passed through her eyes. "Maybe he tried to talk to her and they had a fight. Maybe it was accidental."

He shook his head. "Your mother's injury wasn't accidental." He reached over, touched her shoulder. "But you're right. There could be something else going on that we have no idea about. I'll go talk to him."

* * *

Nicky couldn't sleep. It was long past midnight and she lay in bed, thinking about Cullen and how his eyes seemed to bore right down to her soul. And that kiss. Her body tingled at the memory and her skin felt hot. How could she have let him talk her into staying here?

Punching the pillow, she drove thoughts of him from her mind and forced herself to think of something else. Her suspicions about her uncle sounded silly now. Of course Steve Bosko hadn't killed her mother. Knowing how much his brother loved his wife, killing her would have been like slicing a piece out of her father's heart. Besides, her uncle was a nice man, not the type prone to violence. It didn't make sense. She'd tell Cullen this in the morning. Allan Spidell had to have been the killer. They just had to find proof.

Outside her window, which she'd managed to push open a foot, wind rustled the leaves in the big oak tree in front yard, and moonlight filtered through the branches and danced off the floor. The air smelled fresh, of hay and rich, moist soil.

Down the hallway, she heard a door creak open, then the squeak of footsteps on the old floors. Cullen was up. She heard the bathroom door close. After a minute, the toilet flushed and then water ran in the sink. A minute later, he got back in bed. She imagined him lying down in the bed. Face down? No, he'd sleep on his back, covers off, maybe with his arms crossed over his chest. He probably slept naked.

Do. Not. Go. There.

Thirty minutes later, although it seemed like hours, still unable to sleep, she decided to get up. In the kitchen, she poured a glass of milk, then sat down in the living room, grabbing a wool blanket to throw over her thin nightgown.

She couldn't stay here. Tomorrow, she'd go back to her apartment.

Putting the empty glass of milk on the table, a movement caught her eye. Cullen stood in the doorway, in a white T-shirt and jeans. "Couldn't sleep?"

She hitched up the blanket up to cover her chest. "I'm a terrible sleeper anyway, but I'm trying to figure out what to do." An unexplained lightness came into her chest.

Walking over, he sat down beside her on the sofa. Muscles rippled under the shirt. "And have you decided?"

"I've decided to go back home tomorrow."

"I don't think that's such a good idea."

"Why not?"

"What if Allan Spidell wasn't the person who tried to kill you?" A hint of exasperation laced his tone.

"Who else could it be?"

He remained silent.

She said, "You're risking your career here. If they find out I'm staying here, you could lose your job."

Standing up, he looked at her. "Why don't you let me worry about my career?"

She sucked in a deep breath, a tangle of emotions bouncing around in her head. She felt safe here, and maybe he was right. Maybe Spidell hadn't tried to kill her. Maybe the danger was still out there. But how could she let him shoulder this burden?

She said, "It's still not a good idea."

His lips were pinched. It was something he did when he was annoyed.

She said, "I can go stay with my father, if it makes you feel better."

"How could doing that possibly make me feel better?"

"Why wouldn't it?" She didn't understand.

"Until we find—"

She stood up, the realization hitting her. "You think my father tried to kill me." The blanket dropped to the floor. Flushing, she picked it up, held it so that it covered the front of her body.

"I didn't say that. But you have to know that everybody is a suspect."

"I realize that." She thought about it for a minute. "Do you think I'm trying to cover up for my father?"

"I didn't—"

"Don't lie to me. Do you think I saw my father kill my mother?"

"No, I don't. I think if you had, you wouldn't cover for him. And I certainly wouldn't have you here if I thought that."

Her pulse racing, she sat down again. It was too much. "Well, aren't I special?" She wasted no effort trying to keep the sarcasm out of her voice.

"Do you want me to the lie to you? Tell you what you want to hear?" Anger made his voice thick.

"Okay, I'll bite. What do I want to hear?"

"That Allan Spidell killed your mother and this is over."

She scoffed. "You don't get it, do you? It might put me out of danger, but I'll never find out what happened to my mother. It's not enough knowing who. I have to know why."

"I want to find that out, too. And I have to look at everybody." His eyes flashed like fire.

Tearing her gaze away, she thought about what he'd said. Everybody was a suspect. Maybe not herself, but the list included members of her family. It made sense the cop in him thought like that, but it didn't make it easier to take. And all of a sudden it seemed the ultimate betrayal for her to stay here.

Standing up, she wrapped the blanket around her body. "This was never going to work."

"Would you rather I was dishonest with you?"

"No, and that's exactly why it's not going to work." She walked toward where he stood in the doorway between the living room and hall. "I'm going up to pack. Will you drive me home, or should I call a cab?"

He paused a beat. "Is that what you want?"

She thought about it. "Yes." She owed her father and sister so much, especially now. Staying here would be like stabbing them in the back. "It's the right thing to do. You and I both know it."

"I didn't realize you were so big on doing the right thing."

"What's that supposed to mean?"

"We're talking about you and me, and whether we have a future."

Heat flushed through her body. "How could we possibly have a future?" Just because they both wanted to have sex didn't mean they had a future.

His eyes went dull. "I'll get dressed. I'll be ready when you are." He headed for the stairs, turned to her as he grabbed the newel post at the bottom of the stairway. "I'm on your side, you do realize that?"

"How could you be?"

He blew out a noisy breath. "The fact you have to ask the question says it all." His voice was a growl.

"I do appreciate everything you've done." She meant it. A couple of weeks ago she couldn't have cared less what he thought, but now it seemed utterly important he realize she wasn't an ungrateful bitch.

His brows lowered over his eyes as he glared at her. "Don't say anything."

"What?"

"Don't talk to me," he growled. "I'll drive you home if you promise not to say anything. I mean, not one word." He wet his lips with his tongue. They were very full and she thought about kissing him the previous night, how his lips had felt against hers, soft and silky.

But who the hell did he think he was, telling her not to

talk? She slammed her hands on her hips. "Fine." She spat the word out. "I was going to say you were right about my uncle. Of course the idea is ridiculous, but I won't now. I'll just be a good girl and shut up." She ran an imaginary zipper across her mouth.

Anger flared in his piercing eyes, and some other emotion that colored them as dark as midnight. He licked his lips again and in the next instant backed her against the wall so his face was inches from hers, his hands on the wall on either side of her.

Those lips were very, very close. Her eyes got stuck on them and couldn't look away.

He wasn't touching her. He didn't have to. Heat seared through her and suddenly she could help herself no longer. She wanted those lips. Reaching up, she grabbed his face and pulled his mouth to hers.

His eyes widened in surprise. She nibbled his mouth, then sucked his tongue. Moaning, he lifted her off her feet. She clutched his shoulders and wrapped her legs around him.

Pinned against the wall, his tongue invaded her mouth. Her nightgown bunched up around her waist and she could feel his erection. Heat twisted deep inside her and her legs went weak. She wanted him inside her. Now.

He pulled back, his gaze heated. "Are you sure? You won't regret this in the morning." His voice was low and husky.

"I have no idea what I'll feel in the morning. But I don't care. This is what I want right now."

"It sure beats fighting." His eyes were slits of pleasure.

"Stop talking."

He reached into his pocket and pulled out a condom, and they struggled together to lower his jeans, then he put the condom on.

Need making her shiver, she locked her eyes on his and cried out as he entered her. He began thrusting, his strokes slow at first but then deep and hard as he pinned her against the wall. The smell of him, a sensual mixture of earth and wood and soap, filled her nostrils. She dug her nails into his back, found his mouth again, and sucked his tongue. Waves of pleasure pulsed through her.

She cried out as she came, her orgasm exploding inside her. He thrust once more, then shuddered into her, crying out her name.

CHAPTER SEVENTEEN

Cullen dreamed Nicole was drowning. She had fallen into a river or lake and he dove in, swam around, desperate to find her. When he finally did, her eyes were lifeless and her body limp. Fluorescent fish in colors of red, yellow, and blue swam in formation, weaving in and out around her. As he reached out to grab her, she opened her eyes and smiled. Then a man swam up behind her, a faceless man. As he grabbed her, a whirlpool sucked them in and she was gone.

He woke up, filled with horror. It was one of those vivid, awful dreams that had him convinced it was real. He'd dreamed a version of it a couple of nights ago, with the same faceless man.

When he looked over, Nicole was sleeping soundly beside him, curled tightly into herself. He leaned over, kissed her on the forehead, and then brushed dark hair off her pale cheek. Her hair was soft and smelled clean and sweet.

"You drive me crazy," he whispered into her ear as she slept on.

Ignoring more natural instincts, he decided to let her sleep. He tucked the duvet around her and slipped out of bed.

Downstairs, he put on coffee. As the water sputtered through the filter, he stood at the window, eating a bowl of cereal and watching the rising sun streak across the orange-red sky.

Just don't let her wake up thinking that sleeping with me was a mistake.

Then the anxiety from the dream returned and he realized there were more pressing things to worry about than whether she'd have regrets. His heart constricted. Melodramatic as the dream had been, a faceless man, a killer, lurked out there. Or woman. Someone who had murdered Nicole's mother and now had tried to kill her. It had to be the same person. Instinct told him Allan Spidell hadn't been the killer. That meant he had to find out who was before the killer struck again.

But how?

In the living room, he sat with a second cup of coffee and stared down at the pictures strewn across the table in front of him. On top were the ones Nicole had pointed out the night before, and one with her mother, Allan Spidell, and the other unidentified women and man.

Think.

The identity of the man Lisa Bosko had been having an affair with was still a mystery. Somehow, all roads led back to that. And so far all attempts to find out who the man was had failed. None of her friends from that time claimed to know his name. It seemed odd she hadn't confided in anyone. But he'd bet money the guy had been local.

Looking at the group picture again, he considered one possibility. What if Lisa Bosko had gone out with the guy when they had been teenagers, then met up with him again when she was married?

The uncle was in the picture but no sign of Nicky's father. The uncle would be able to identify the other man. And the women. If Steve Bosko couldn't tell him, then maybe one of the women could point to somebody.

He would start with Steve Bosko.

First things first. Cullen was working for the next couple of evenings, and he didn't want Nicole here on her own. Flipping through his phone contacts, he stopped at Anna. She was working days. He rang her cell phone, explained the situation. After considerable reluctance, he managed to convince her to let Nicole stay at her place for the next couple of nights.

"You owe me big time," she said. "Mullen will have both our necks on a platter if she finds out."

"Whatever you want, Anna, whatever you want. By the way, any news from the inspection of Nicole's car?"

"Not yet, but I may get something later this morning." She hung up without waiting for a reply.

At 8:30, with still no noise from Nicole, he wrote a note telling her where he was going and he would be back soon. He didn't mention the new sleeping arrangements.

* * *

Nicky woke with a start and sat up, for a long moment unsure where she was, until memories of the previous night came crashing back. A quick look around confirmed she was alone.

In Cullen's bed.

Oh, God.

Ears perked, she couldn't hear anything. After a minute, still nothing. Maybe he'd gotten up, went downstairs, and then fell asleep on the sofa. He'd need sleep after the energy expended last night. She'd read somewhere sex used about as much energy as a short jog. Well, they'd run the equivalent of a marathon. While sprinting. Nothing short of hibernation would do.

Warmth crept up her neck into her face and heat stirred in her lower belly.

Flopping back on the bed, she peeked under the sheets. Cullen's scent and the smell of sex wafted up. She was butt-ass naked. The feel of his arms on her was strong, burning her skin. Nothing had mattered, just the two of them.

But of course it wasn't just the two of them. It seemed an utterly irresponsible thing to have done, looking at it in the cold light of day.

Getting out of bed, she tiptoed down the hall to her room and slipped into a sweater and jeans. The house was still silent as she crept downstairs. Cullen wasn't asleep on the sofa. In the kitchen, she found a note on the table, telling her he'd gone to see her uncle to find out who the other people in the photos were. It was signed, simply, Cullen, and her breath hitched. But what did she expect? A profession of undying love?

Get real.

She made fresh coffee and ate the rest of the yogurt from a container in the fridge. She'd had another dream last night, a variation on one she'd had a few times since she remembered the near-drowning at the lake. But last night another detail had appeared. Her blood chilled at the memory. In the dream, Karina had pushed her off the dock, then stared down into the water at her.

Shaking it off, she turned on the radio to hear a woman interviewing a park ranger about a possible cull of wolves in a state park. When the interview finished, she headed to the bathroom for a shower.

Later, she called her sister, wanting to hear her voice, to hear that everything was all right. Karina didn't answer, so she left a message and had another cup of coffee. Half an hour later, feeling restless, she was contemplating a walk when her sister called back.

Karina said, "Where in the heck were you? We went to the hospital and you were gone."

She ignored the scolding tone in her sister's voice. "Staying at a friend's place."

"You could have let told us. We were worried."

"I'm telling you now."

"Where are you?"

She hesitated. "I'm staying at a farm on Beck Road. The number I called you on is my new cell number, if you want to reach me."

"What are you doing today?" The anger was gone from her voice, replaced by a pleading tone. "I need to see you. I'm worried about Dad."

"What's wrong?"

"His blood pressure is through the roof. He's worried sick about you. Can you come over?"

She was still feeling jittery, didn't want to go out. "I'm sorry, I can't. Not today."

"Why not? What's so important that it can't wait until tomorrow?" Karina's voice had risen. "I'm carrying all the heavy lifting with Dad here. You could at least think about him."

Nicky swallowed, didn't say anything. There was something new in Karina's tone, a kind of desperation.

"Just for an hour or so. I could come pick you up. Please, I need you, sweetie."

The pleading note in Karina's voice couldn't be ignored. She sighed. "All right."

"Give me your address and I can be there in an hour."

She gave Karina directions and her sister pulled into the lane in a sports car an hour later, just after before noon.

Nicky locked up, then got in the car. It smelled new and seemed to have as many dials as the average aircraft. "Nice ride," she said.

"It's not mine. The dealership let me have it for a couple of days. I'm still deciding if I like it."

It looked expensive, too expensive for someone on a nurse's salary, but Nicky didn't know much about cars. Maybe she'd get a loan from their father.

"Whose house is this?" Karina asked.

"A friend's."

"It'd kind of a dump, isn't it?" Karina's lip curled up in distaste. "And it smells out here."

"It's quite lovely, actually. It needs work, but it's got good bones. And the smell's not so bad."

"What are you, a real estate agent?" Karina's eyes narrowed. "Whose is it?" Her sister was persistent if nothing else.

"Cullen Fraser owns it." She considered lying but Karina would be able to tell.

"The detective?" When Nicky nodded, her eyes widened. "Isn't that against the rules?"

"That's me, always breaking the rules." She smiled, shutting down the topic. "Drive on, sister."

The cows were out again, about thirty big Holsteins. Behind them, across the field, a tall silver silo with a dome-shaped top dwarfed two leafy trees and a red barn beside it.

Nicky remembered she forgotten her phone, and was about to ask Karina to go back for it, but decided not to. She'd left Cullen a note and she'd be back in an hour or two anyway.

Karina said, "I hope you're hungry. We've got a pot of soup on."

Nicky turned to look at her sister, "How are you doing?"

"I'm okay. The last few days have been stressful, what with your accident and Dad not feeling well, but I'm managing. It's awful to say, but I feel better now that Allan Spidell's dead." She gave Nicky a long look. "Dad found out somehow that you went to see him. He was very angry."

"At me?"

"More so at Spidell and the fact that he tried to kill you."

"I don't know where dad gets his information. We can't be sure Spidell tried to kill me."

Karina looked at Nicky, shocked. "Who else would it be?"

Nicky bit her lip. "It could have been an accident."

Karina said, "You and I both know that isn't true. Of course it was Allan Spidell. He killed mom, too. We may never know why, but we'll just have to live with that. You realize that, don't you? Your detective can be the best detective in the world, but unless he can make dead men talk, we won't know."

"He's not my detective."

"Well, you know what I mean."

Tears stung her eyes. Karina was right, but it hurt to hear it said out loud.

A large semi-truck drove up behind them. Karina slowed and pulled to the side of the lane to let it pass, then reached over, rubbed her hand. "I'm sorry, sweetie."

"Sweetie" had been Karina's pet name for her when she was little. She forgot when Karina had stopped using it, but it was likely when Nicky'd stopped being a sweetie and had started turning bad. But now something about Karina's smile and her use of the term just felt contrived.

Nicky pulled her hand back. "Do you ever think about moving away?"

"Funny you mention that. I have a job offer in New York, a good one."

"Wow. What is it?"

"It's at a hospital. A unit manager for a medical-surgery re-hab unit. Thirty-two beds. It's right up my alley."

"You would be great, Karina."

She smiled grimly. "I haven't decided whether to take it. That's one of the things I wanted to talk to you about. I don't know what to do."

"But you want to take it?"

She nodded. "I think I do, but I want to be sure. I've lived here my whole life."

She didn't want to leave their father. Karina didn't say it, but that was the reason. Nicky said, "He can look after himself."

"I just feel protective of him. It's hard to explain." Her hands were tight on the steering wheel.

"But are you happy?"

Karina didn't answer and it occurred to Nicky again that she was the lucky one. She wasn't as put together, as successful, and she'd made plenty of mistakes. But they were her mistakes. Karina lived too much on the straight and narrow to have the chance to make many mistakes. At the same time, she had to live up to their father's expectations. The stress showed in the lines around her mouth and eyes, lines that a woman who'd turned thirty not long ago shouldn't have had.

They pulled off the highway and onto the road leading up to their father's house. A few miles in, Nicky caught sight of the lake and a cold hand reached in and squeezed her heart. The accident was too fresh in her mind. She could feel the water on her body, her lungs screaming for air, smell the slippery seaweed in her hair, taste it in her mouth. Clutching the seat, she squeezed her eyes shut.

Karina stopped the car. "Nicole, are you all right?"

Her head in her hands, Nicky fought panic. Blood swooshed in her head and her pulse raced. It all felt like everything was going to pieces.

Karina clutched her hand. "Nicole?"

She tried to talk but words wouldn't come. She thought of

almost drowning in the lake as a child and wondered if her dream held the truth, if Karina had tried to drown her. What was she doing in the car?

"Nicole, sweetie?" Karina tugged on her arm.

She opened her eyes and looked at Karina, who stared at her, wide-eyed. "Are you okay?"

Nodding, she concentrated on taking deep breaths. Of course that wasn't how it had happened. *Get a grip.*

Karina had stopped the car just before the crash site. Ahead, a twisted and broken section of guardrail showed where the car had broken through.

Hugging herself, she closed her eyes so she wouldn't have to see Karina. Or the lake. She wanted to call Cullen, to hear his voice, but she'd forgotten the stupid phone.

"Nicole?" Karina tugged her arm.

She managed to recover her voice enough to say, "I'm fine. Let's just go, okay?"

CHAPTER EIGHTEEN

Cullen found Steve Bosko at the side of his house, where he was building a retaining wall to level off an area in the yard where it sloped steeply down to the woods surrounding the property. Bosko grabbed a concrete block with one hand and set it down gently on the concrete footing. He was a wiry man, smaller than his older brother, but his arm muscles bulged and his power belied his size. This wasn't a guy who ran his business sitting behind a desk all the time.

Spotting Cullen, he wiped the sweat off his brow with his forearm and climbed up the small embankment. He brushed his hands together to get rid of the loose dirt, then shook Cullen's hand with a firm grip. He smelled of damp earth and sweat.

They walked up to the patio at the back of the house, where Bosko poured a glass of water from a pitcher on a patio table. "Would you like some?" When Cullen shook his head, they sat down in chairs beside the table. The air was still, with no wind at all, but the musky smell of the lake hung in the air. The dully gray water was just visible through a bank of fir trees near shore.

The spot where Nicole's car had crashed into the water was several miles up the road, on the other side of his brother's place. Cullen sucked in a breath, suddenly chilled by fear. He shouldn't have left her alone. Maybe he should ask for some time off. Then he could keep a closer eye on her and investigate the case on his own time. And the chief wouldn't be able to pull him off the case.

Bosko said, "What can I do for you?"

Cullen took the picture of the high school students out of a manila envelope and set it on the table. "I was wondering if you could identify any of these people in the photo."

Bosko leaned forward, took a look, then pointed a dirty finger at the man with his hair in a ponytail hair. "That's Chris Vial. He moved away, not sure where. He only lived here for a year, his father was in the military and they moved around a lot. The other guy is Allan Spidell and then there's me."

"You didn't stay in contact with Vial?"

"No, sorry. I'm not sure how you'd track him down, either, other than, like I said, his father was in the military." He straightened. "Nola might know. I think there was some sort of family connection. They were second cousins or something. We only found out about that later, when I met Nola. She wasn't from here."

Nicky made a note to ask Nola about Chris Vial. "And the girls?"

Bosko pointed to a short girl with dark frizzy hair. "Her

name is Wanda Mackie. I went out with her for a while. She married some guy from Canada. I think they're living in Montreal. She might've changed her name when she married."

Writing down the names, Cullen nodded encouragement.

It took him longer minute to come up with the other woman's name. "The girl beside Wanda is Noor Baloche," he said. "No idea where she is. We kind of lost touch."

"And the other girl?"

Taking a sip of water, he looked at the picture again. "I can't remember. I wasn't friends with her." He scratched his head. "I think she still lives around her. She looks familiar. Or maybe I'm mixing her up with somebody else. It's been a long time, decades ago. Why? Is it important?"

"I'd like to talk to them, see if they can tell us anything that might be relevant to the investigation."

He raised his eyebrows. "How could they? The photo was taken a long time ago, our last year of high school, at least a decade before Lisa disappeared. I don't think she had contact with any of them, other than Spidell, of course, after that."

"And yourself."

"Of course, and myself." He shifted in his chair.

"Did she have a relationship with Spidell or this Vial guy? Something that might have resumed after she was married?"

"No." His cleared his throat.

"You seem pretty sure."

"I think I would have known." Bosko drew back, eyed Cullen warily.

Cullen watched him closely. "How close were you to her?"

His eyes darkened. "We were good friends. We hung out in the same group together." He pointed at the picture. "She wasn't interested in either of those guys."

"Who was she interested in? Do you have any idea who that man—or woman—might have been?"

Finished with the water, he held the glass in a white-knuckle grip. "Why is it so important? What if it has nothing to do with what happened?"

An edge in Bosko's tone struck Cullen. He tensed. Maybe Nicole hadn't been so wrong about her uncle, after all. He said, "It wasn't you?"

"Wasn't me what?" He set the glass down.

"Did you ever go out with Lisa Bosko?"

Bosko stood up suddenly, knocking over his chair. He walked to the edge of the patio, swinging his hands, then turned around.

Cullen was already standing, ready.

But Bosko sat down, and when he looked up his face was a mottled red. After a long moment, he said, "I did, yes, before she was married. In high school. When that picture was taken." A dark shadow crossed his face. "But I would never have hurt her."

Cullen waited, sucked in a lungful of cool air.

Bosko said, "I wanted to marry her. That was the plan. We were supposed to get married when she came back from college. But she ended up picking my brother instead."

"Were you angry about that?"

His eyes were bleak. "Anger isn't the word. More disappointed. It happened very quickly." He crossed his arms over his chest, eyed Cullen warily. "But you've got to believe me, I would never have hurt her."

His eyes glistening with tears, he covered his face with his hands. Dirt and flakes of dried concrete smeared his forearms. After a moment, he put his hands down and looked up. "She made her decision and I accepted it."

Something clicked in place. Sitting down again, he said, "Did your brother find out about the affair?"

Eyes widening, Bosko seemed ready to protest but instead slumped back in his chair. When he finally spoke, his voice was flat. "No, he didn't. But it had been over for a couple of years.

It had nothing to do with what happened to her."

Cullen waited.

"She didn't want to leave Jim; she didn't want to break up the family. And neither of us wanted to carry on the way it was. It felt too"—he searched for the word—"too dirty."

"Are you sure your brother didn't know?"

From Bosko came a quick nod. "Absolutely. If he had, he would have disowned me. Do you have to tell him now? It would kill him." His voice cracked.

Steve Bosko seemed unaware he had just supplied his own motive for killing Lisa Bosko. If she'd told her husband, that would have been the end of Steve Bosko's relationship with his brother.

Cullen said, "You should have come forward."

"What good would it have done? I didn't kill her. I would never have hurt her. And I didn't know who this guy was. If it all came out, it would only hurt Jim more. You have to understand, Jim comes across as a really strong person but he isn't. He's near broken."

Frowning, he studied Bosko. "Did you talk to her on the phone in the months before she died?"

When Bosko nodded, Cullen said, "What was she scared of?"

"I didn't get the impression she was scared. She was worried about something, I know that. I begged her to tell me what it was, but she wouldn't." He thought about it some more. "She kept talking about Nicole, about how she had to do the right thing for Nicole."

His gut hardening, Cullen said, "What else did she say about Nicole? What was the right thing?"

"I couldn't get it out of her. I wanted to help her, but she wouldn't let me. She told me that if I said a word to anyone she would never speak to me again." A tear rolled down his cheek. "I should never have listened to her. If I had, she might still be alive."

With that, he doubled over, his body wracked by sobs.

* * *

When Karina pulled into the driveway of their father's house a few minutes later, Nicky's heart rate had slowed enough for her to believe she was no longer in danger of passing out.

Karina parked in front of the garage, then turned to Nicky, her eyes dark and watchful. "Are you okay?"

She nodded. Her hands still shook and she was shivering. A big mistake it had been to agree to come.

For a second, Karina's eyes hardened and appeared almost hostile, as if she knew what Nicky was thinking, but then it was gone, and Nicky supposed she'd imagined it. Her sister loved her, always had. Someday she'd ask Karina what had happened, once she'd figured out how to broach the topic. Kids sometimes did crazy things. She was a prime example. It was their behavior as adults that counted.

Their father was raking a thin scattering of leaves into a small pile on the front lawn. Reaching for the door handle, Karina said, "Some things never change."

Nicky returned her smile. Their father was a perfectionist by nature. It made him an excellent doctor, some said the best in the county, but his obsession with his lawn bordered on fanaticism. They'd once joked about staging an intervention but her father hadn't seen the humor.

Karina said, "He still mows it every four days and he's been out a few times now raking up leaves, even though they haven't even started falling off the trees yet."

Nicky imitated his voice. "Yes, well, we can't leave them to rot on the grass."

Chuckling, Karina shot her a smile, then got out the car.

Nicky took a deep breath. Still rattled, she thought her father would likely be happier outdoors raking leaves than inside with them. Opening the door, she stepped out of the car and joined her father and sister on the lawn. He still looked tired, although his eyes were no longer red.

He said, "I'll join you inside in a minute."

In the kitchen, Karina lifted the lid off the soup on the stove and gave it a stir with a wooden spoon. The smell of chicken noodle soup wafted across the room. Karina left the lid off, then got some whole wheat rolls out of the breadbox and butter from the refrigerator.

Reaching for glasses in the cupboard, Nicky said, "Do you think dad's going to be okay? He's not depressed, is he?"

Karina smeared butter on a roll. "He just needs more time."

"Maybe he should see someone."

"You're probably right, but I don't know if he'd agree. I'm at my wit's end, to tell you the truth." Karina's brow creased. "I was going to tell him about the job offer, but now might be a good time."

A few minutes later their father came in through the back door. He took off his shoes and sat down in the family room. He made noises suggesting he should have helped with lunch, but Karina shrugged it off and carried a tray with steaming soup mugs and rolls into the family room.

As Nicky sat down, she noticed a framed picture of her mother and father on the mantel she was sure she hadn't ever seen before.

Karina saw her look. "Dad thought it was about time we displayed some pictures of Mom."

Their father gave a grim smile. "I'm sorry to you both that I didn't do more to make your mother's presence felt in the house."

Nicky and Karina exchanged a quick look. Karina said, "It's perfectly understandable, Dad."

They chatted some more, mainly about work, before her father said, "I heard about Allan Spidell. I can't say I'm sorry, especially after he tried to kill you. You should have told me.

You know I would have found out anyway. There's not much in this town I don't know about."

Nicky put her half-eaten sandwich down. "I wish I was surer he was the one who was responsible."

"Of course he was. Who else would do it?" He dismissed her comment with a flick of his wrist. "Did the police confirm that he tampered with your car?"

"I don't think they know yet. The thing that gets me, I don't understand the reason."

Her father shrugged. "Don't try to overanalyze everything. You went to see him, right? Maybe he felt threatened."

An undercurrent of impatience in his tone suggested he didn't want to discuss it further.

Karina put down her glass of milk and eyed her father steadily. "Do you think Mom had an affair with him?"

Nicky, surprised Karina had asked, waited for the answer.

He closed his eyes. "I don't know. I know at one time they were friends. I guess it's possible. We may never know what exactly happened and we have to be prepared to live with that."

That would be hard for her father, who liked loose ends tidied up. But the stress seemed to be getting to him.

Nicky said, with a mind to changing the topic, "I'll bring back the other photo albums. I'm sure you'd like to look through them also."

Her father said, "No hurry, but it would be nice to have a peek."

A few minutes later, she picked up a photo album sitting on the coffee table in front of her. Karina was clearing away the lunch dishes, having refused her help, and was in the kitchen making coffee. The photos in this album were like some of the ones in the collection at Cullen's place. Looking at them, her insides twisted. Would she ever be able to let go of her anger and move forward? Right now, it didn't seem possible.

She closed her eyes, pinched the bridge of her nose. But her father was right. She had to accept that the full truth might never be known. Believe Allan Spidell had been the murderer.

On the table in front of her, the album was open to the photo of her mother in the yellow dress standing by the fence. She was looking at the camera, an enigmatic expression on her face, as though she was thinking of some far-off place. It had been her favorite photo of her mother, until she'd learned her had mother had been killed in that dress. Cullen had wanted to know when it had been taken.

She showed the picture to her father as Karina came with coffee. "When was this taken? I remember that dress."

Karina said, "I don't remember it."

Nicky said, "It's the only piece of clothing of Mom's I remember." She didn't want to mention it was also the dress she was wearing when she was murdered. She doubted Cullen had told them.

Her father looked over. "Let me think. I think it was in the spring. That was the only time she ever wore it." He wiped his eyes.

She said, "Oh, Dad, I didn't mean to upset you."

"It's okay. Memories are good."

"But are you sure it was the spring?"

"Is it important?"

Ignoring him, a wisp of memory, thin and light as air, surfaced. Her mother in that dress on the front step. Sitting back, she tried to tease out the details.

This time it was Karina who spoke. "Nicole? What's wrong?"

Tension building in her, she studied their faces. The memory was faded, like a sepia-tinted photograph, but one detail was clear as a blinding light. "She wore it when she saw me off to school. I can picture her on the front step, waving to me."

Both just looked at her, saying nothing.

"It wouldn't have been the spring. I wasn't in school until that fall." Her throat went dry. "I think it was the last day I saw her." It made sense, since she'd started school not long before her mother disappeared.

Karina raised her eyebrows. "Is this important? Show it to me again."

She passed Karina the photo album. Her father put his head down. When he raised it, his face was flushed and his lips had flattened into a hard line.

Karina said, "You're right. It was in September, just before school started. I do remember it now because I was with her when she bought it. I got an outfit for the first day of school. She said the dress was for a special occasion. What was that, Dad? Your anniversary?"

A chill spread over Nicky's skin. "Your anniversary? You had the day off, didn't you, Dad?"

In a horrible instant, an idea started to gel. Her mother had worn the dress the day she had gone for an anniversary lunch with Nicky's father. The day she had been murdered.

Not the next day, when her father was at work.

Her father stared at her, not saying anything.

Karina stared at him. "Dad, what is it? What's wrong?"

Her father stood suddenly, walked out of the room and down the hallway. A moment later, the bathroom door closed.

Karina glared at her. "You're upsetting him. What does it matter what she was wearing?"

Their father returned, walked into the kitchen, opened a drawer, and then stood at the breakfast bar, that unfocused look in his eyes.

Standing up, Nicky walked to the kitchen to face him across from the breakfast bar. She clasped her hands to keep them from shaking. "You weren't at work the day Mom was murdered, were you?"

Karina walked up to Nicky, grabbed her roughly by the arm. "What are you talking about?"

Ignoring her, Nicky looked at her father. "What happened?" Her voice croaked, but she pushed on. "Was she going to leave you?"

Not saying anything, her father watched her for a moment, his eyes cold and his lips thinned into a bitter smile.

Then he reached in the kitchen drawer and pulled out a gun.

CHAPTER NINETEEN

A cold sweat broke out everywhere on Nicky's body and she felt the floor sway beneath her. Her father had never had a gun. He'd been antigun his whole life. Or so she'd thought. How could she have been so wrong in so many ways?

All those years, she thought her mother had taken off, abandoned them. But her father had killed her mother. And had tried to kill her. Would now kill her.

Karina leaned her elbows on the counter, steadying herself, then put her head in her hands. "I don't understand."

"He killed Mom on Tuesday, the day he was off work for the anniversary lunch, not the Wednesday. But he told everybody that Wednesday was the last day we saw her, because he had an alibi for that day."

A mixture of anger and fear churning inside her, Nicky turned to her father. "Why?" she demanded.

His face was a mask, hard and vicious, unrecognizable as her father. He opened his mouth to speak but the doorbell rang.

Her father started, looked quickly at Karina. "Karina, send whoever it is away." Karina stood frozen in place. "Karina!"

Lifting her head, Karina's eyes looked cold and lifeless.

"Go!" James Bosko barked.

Clenching her fists, Nicky waited for Karina to refuse, to challenge her father.

Instead, Karina brushed a hand across her face to wipe away tears, then walked like a robot to the door.

Blood pounded in Nicky's ears. Her father. Now her sister, too. Sweat trickled down her spine. Her father's icy eyes bore into her.

He hates you. Loathes you. Why?

A voice came from the hallway. It was loud, insistent. A man. Cullen.

She froze, said a silent prayer for him to go away.

"Keep quiet," her father hissed, pointing the gun at her.

Nicky bit her lip as tears splashed down her face.

Just seconds later, Karina returned with Cullen in tow. His eyes widened when he saw the gun in James Bosko's hand, then his gaze darted around the room until he found Nicky.

Her father barked at Karina, "Couldn't you get rid of him?"

Karina seemed to be in a daze. Looking down, she walked slowly to her father's side, where she stood listlessly.

Her father walked over to Cullen, searched him for a gun. Finding none, he gestured with his own toward Nicky, who stood in the middle of the family room near the sofa. Cullen walked over, took her hand in his, and shot her a grim smile.

She had to buy time, figure out a way to save Cullen. But how? Keep her father talking.

She said, "Why? At least tell me why."

His eyes narrowed into mean, angry slits. "Why do you think? Your mother was running around on me."

"You said it was over; you had reconciled."

He huffed. "What do you take me for? I couldn't just pretend it didn't happen."

Nicky took a step closer. "I certainly didn't take you for a murderer."

Her father pointed the gun at her. "Stay where you are."

Cullen took a step closer so he was beside her. "What do you plan to do now? Kill us both? You'll never get away with it."

James Bosko smirked. "Of course I will." He turned to Karina. "Get the twine out of the drawer in the kitchen. Tie him up. Hurry up."

As Karina walked to the kitchen, Nicky gave a sharp intake of breath. "And the man Mom had the affair with? Did you kill him, too?"

He waited until Karina had finished tying their hands behind their backs to continue. "I'll get to that. I imagine with you two gone he'll be waiting for it."

Cullen said, "Your own brother? You'd kill your own brother?"

Her breath catching, Nicky turned to Cullen. "What?" It couldn't be true.

Cullen said, "Your mother and your uncle had a relationship in high school. They even planned to get married, but when she came back from college, your father won her away."

Her father said, "Did he brag about that to you? He had to have everything, didn't he?"

Cullen said, "Your whole lives were one big competition, but to hear him tell it, you were the one who drove it."

Her father's lips curled in disgust. "Little Stevie had to win. And every time, he had to shove it in my face. Well, I was going to show him."

Cullen inched closer. "Especially when you knew how much he loved her."

Bile rose in Nicky's throat. All her father's talk about brotherly love and the importance of family relationships. It had just been so much air. Why did he kill his wife rather than his brother? To make him suffer? She wanted to scream.

Cullen turned to Karina, who stood ashen-faced at his side, not moving. "What did you know about this?"

James Bosko answered for her. "She didn't know I killed your mother, if that's what you're worried about. She just helped with my alibi. Unlike Nicky, she knows the meaning of loyalty."

Nicky looked at Karina, tried to summon pity for her sister but was left with something closer to disgust. Her father wasn't even going to allow Karina to speak for herself. He had taken total control over her, as he had done her entire life. It was as if she wasn't even in the room.

Cullen slid closer yet, standing about four feet from her father. He said, "And now you're prepared to shoot your own daughter?"

"Who says she's mine?" Her father spat the words out.

Nicky gasped, froze. A heavy weight descended on her chest. James Bosko said, "Steve is her father, not me. I had a suspicion about it, but Lisa didn't admit it until the end."

Steely eyes glanced toward Nicky. "He doesn't know, in case you're wondering."

Cullen said, "Was that why Lisa was scared for Nicole? She thought you were going to take revenge by killing Nicole?"

James Bosko huffed. "I'm glad I didn't. It turned out to be so much more fun watching her make a mess of her life."

Nicky closed her eyes, tried to block the cruel, hurtful words. So many things made sense now. She had made such a mess of her life; she had made it so easy for him.

Cullen said, "Except her life isn't such a mess, is it?" He glanced at her, his eyes full of warmth and love. "That must really bug you."

James Bosko walked over to the back door, then motioned with the gun for them to follow. On his face was a look of mock sorrow. "Not really, because her time is up and so is yours. Let's go."

She said, "Where are you taking us?"

"The boat. This time I'll make sure the job is finished."

Cullen repeated, "You'll never get away with it."

A ghastly smile formed on James Bosko's lips. "I wouldn't be so sure. It shouldn't be so hard to pin this on Steve—especially when he's dead." He spoke with discouraging calmness.

"Please, Dad, please don't do this," she begged.

Her father—the man she had thought was her father—laughed coldly. "I'm not your father. I never was. I've got one daughter and that's enough."

Nicky swallowed hard. He would force them into his boat, take them out to the lake, kill them, and then pin the murders on his own brother. A fierce kind of anger grew in her, an anger fueled by humiliation, disgust at his depravity, and the knowledge he would kill again. And get away with it again.

He'd done such a great job of pretending, pretending he'd wanted to find out who had killed his wife. The tears, the pleas for justice, they were just ploys. The man who stood before her now, his eyes cold as ice, skin stretched to a snarl, looked like another person. But he was the real James Bosko, stripped of artifice. The man she'd thought was her father had been a fake. He had always hated her, she realized now with crystal clarity. She'd thought their difficulties were because, unlike Karina, she had rebelled. But he had wanted her to fail. That had been his revenge.

James Bosko stood to the side of the door. "Let's go."

A move had to be made soon if she had any hope of stopping his cold-blooded plan. She stepped toward the door. Cullen followed behind her. Karina stood to the side, avoiding eye contact.

Her whole body trembling, she forced herself forward. Two more steps and she was in front of the door. James Bosko pointed the gun at her with a steady hand. It was close enough to reach.

She stopped, met those cold eyes. "Please, Dad." Hoping to distract him, she injected a pleading note in her voice. "Can't we just talk about this?"

He smirked, then motioned with the gun to the door again. *Now or never.*

She lunged at him in a furious panic, reaching for the hand that held the gun. Screamed.

But he must have been prepared for her attack, because he was too quick. He wrenched his hand away and pulled the trigger.

***

Cullen had no time to react. When Nicole lunged for the gun, letting out an almost animalistic roar, Bosko reacted with lightning speed. Cullen shoved Nicole to the floor a split second before Bosko yanked his hand away and pulled back on the trigger.

It was a budget version Smith & Wesson, small but deadly. The gunshot was deafening and he felt a kick in his right shoulder, the force of the impact at such close range spinning him around and flinging him back against the sofa behind him.

He was stunned for a moment, then looked at his shoulder and saw blood. Not enough to suggest an artery had been clipped, but enough to know he'd been hit.

Nicole, eyes wide in horror, rushed to his side. He breathed deep, tried to offer a reassuring smile. "It's all right. I'm okay." Except for the fact he'd just been shot, was tied up, and that they were about to die.

Bosko grunted triumphantly. "Try again and I'll put a bullet in your head right here."

Tears pooled in Nicole's eyes as she examined his shoulder. She glared at Karina. "Help him, for God's sake."

Karina stiffened and started to move, but her father put out a hand and held her back, then looked at him and Nicole. "Let's get moving," he growled.

His shoulder didn't hurt much, but it was hard to move because his hands were bound too tightly behind his back. He couldn't have done it better himself. They stumbled to the door.

Nicole glanced at him. Tears flowed down her cheeks. "I'm so sorry," she whispered.

His breath caught in his throat. "It's not your fault."

They walked out the door, and started across the rocks toward the lake. He glanced behind to see Bosko following them. Karina walked behind him, her movements mechanical, her expression dull, as if the life had gone out of her like air from a balloon.

"What are we going to do?" Nicole whispered. Her eyes were wide and she looked scared, but there was still fight left in her.

He ran through the options. It didn't look good. Their captor was armed and had an accomplice. He was injured. He was tied up. Nobody knew they were here, so the possibility of rescue was almost nil. Cullen had told Anna he was going to see Steve Bosko, but he hadn't updated her on his visit right after to James Bosko. He wasn't even on the clock until later in the day. That was hours from now. They wouldn't know anything was wrong.

His blood chilled. He and Nicole would be long dead by then, their bodies dumped in the lake.

But he had to try something. At least he could try to make sure Nicole survived. Up ahead was the dock, a wooden platform built over the rocks and extending about eight feet over the water. A white motorboat was tied to the side. It was about fifteen feet long, with room for five people at the most. It must have been used recently, because the outboard was in the water.

His shoulder was starting to hurt. It was a nagging pain, but bearable.

Bosko pushed him toward the boat. "Get in."

Nicole sat down, swung her legs over the side of the boat, and climbed in. He followed her and they shuffled to the back and sat down.

Bosko stepped into the boat, followed by Karina. Bosko sat in front behind the steering wheel. Karina sat in the other seat and took the gun when he handed it to her. He said, "Don't let them move. If either of them does, put a bullet in both of them."

Karina sat sideways, her arm draped across the back of the seat, the gun in her hand pointed at them. An empty look had dulled her eyes but she had her finger on the trigger. She was on autopilot, and her father had the controls.

Bosko turned on the ignition and the boat kicked to life. The lake was shaped like an *S*, trees all around. The few houses built on the lake had been set back closer to the road. Only somebody standing on the shoreline could see them, and it didn't look like anybody was out.

He glanced at Nicole, who shivered in her seat and glared at her sister. The wind was picking up, and cold, choppy water splashed against the hull.

What in the hell were they going to do? They could try jumping out, but their chances of getting shot were pretty high. Never mind trying to swim with your hands tied behind your back.

They were halfway down the lake, Bosko steering the boat close to the shoreline, but going along at a decent clip. Once in a while he glanced over his shoulder, but Karina, avoiding her sister's glare, kept the gun pointed in their direction.

Tears stained Nicole's pale cheeks. "I'm sorry."

Leaning toward her, he kissed her cheek. "You have nothing to be sorry about. But we've got to figure out a way to get out of this."

"We're close enough to shore. We have to jump. Can you get untied?"

"I'm working on it," he lied. There was no way he could get untied. "Almost done." He met her eyes. They were huge. Torture to look at and think it would all be over for them, just when things were getting started. "As soon as he slows down. We'll count to three, then go together." He'd wait, throw himself at Karina. At least give Nicole a fighting chance.

The boat hit a big wave with a smack. His shoulder hurt now, the pain searing.

A minute later, Bosko pulled into a sheltered cove and cut the engine.

Cullen tried again to untie the rope behind his back. It cut deep into his wrists as he spread his hands. The rope was too tight.

They were close enough to shore that Nicole might be able to get to land without being shot. It wasn't much of a chance, but it was better than nothing. Karina had the gun pointed at him, ready to fire. Her hands were shaking now, and an odd look came over her face, something like panic, her eyes bulging, as if she were just realizing what was happening.

Cullen stood up, put himself in front of Nicole, spread his legs to steady himself as the boat pitched in the choppy water. "Get ready," he whispered over his shoulder. "One, two—"

James Bosko got to his feet and reached down to take the gun from Karina, who was still sitting. Moaning now, she jerked her hand away.

"Karina, give it to me." Bosko held out his hand, his voice calm, assured.

Turning toward him, Karina's eyes were flat and emotionless. As he stepped towards her, she pointed the gun up at him, squeezed her eyes shut for a moment, and then opened them.

And shot her father in the chest.

CHAPTER TWENTY

For Nicky, the rest of the day passed in a blur. Her father was dead. Cullen was rushed to the hospital in an ambulance. Karina was taken into custody.

She faced hours of interviews at the police station, only stopping when she thought her head was about to explode. After that, she grabbed a cab to the hospital, only to find Cullen's room swarming with people. Most of them looked like cops, but they weren't there in any official capacity; she could tell because there was too much laughter for that.

She was feeling wretched and desperately wanted to see him, to hold on to him and never let go. It had only been possible to get through the day by thinking about Cullen, about how much she needed him. And loved him.

But she couldn't face more people right now. Just as she turned to go, Anna Ackerman came out of the room, saw her, and walked over. "Nicole, I didn't expect to see you here. I mean, with everything's that happened. Are you sure you're okay? You don't look it."

"I've been better," she said, offering a small smile. "How is Cullen?"

"He's going to be fine." She reached for Nicky's hand. "Come on in, he'll want to see you."

Nicky said, "I'll come back tomorrow, when it's not so busy."

Somebody inside the room laughed, a big, booming sound. A nurse stood up at the nursing station, caught Ackerman's eye.

Ackerman said, "I'd better go tell them to keep it down if they don't want to get thrown out. He'll be out tomorrow, by the way. He was lucky. It was a clean exit and apparently the nurses are lining up for home-care duty."

She rolled her eyes. "I'll bet they are."

"I'm picking him up in the morning, so give him a call in the afternoon if you want to talk to him."

Nicky thanked Ackerman and left. She took a cab home, where she heated up some tomato soup from a can for supper, then had a long bath. Emily phoned as she was toweling off. Her friend, aghast, had just heard the news on the radio. They talked for half an hour, Nicky filling her in on the details, including the possibility that her uncle might be her real father. She'd only just managed to convince Emily to not get in her car and drive four hours to Nicky's house that night.

When she hung up, Nicky thought about calling her uncle, but decided to put it off until the next day. It all seemed too much. She'd spoken to him briefly at the police station and although he knew his brother had killed Lisa Bosko, he hadn't been told Nicky might be his daughter.

Sleep didn't come until three in the morning, and when it did, it was filled with crazy, frightening dreams. When she woke at nine in the morning, the first thing that popped into her head was having another memorial service for her mother, something small and private and not tainted by the presence of James Bosko.

Her morning was busy, with a short visit to a psychiatric wing of the hospital where Karina was being held under guard. A call to her uncle followed that, but she didn't end up telling him about his possible paternity, chickening out at the last minute. She wanted to see Cullen first, maybe have him tag along to break the news. What if her uncle balked at the prospect? She didn't want to handle that alone.

At two p.m., she got in the car and drove out to Cullen's house, crossing her fingers nobody else would be around. Her heart was pounding in her chest when she drove past the fields on the road to his house. When she arrived, there was a car parked in the driveway, not his but a late-model sedan. Getting shot had made him Mr. Popularity.

She walked across the driveway, the gravel crunching beneath her shoes, and knocked on the back door. This time she wasn't going to be deterred from getting him to herself.

The smiling woman who opened the door a few seconds later was the blond television reporter.

Nicky felt a pain in her chest, almost unbearable, as if she were being torn apart inside. The ex-girlfriend who obviously wasn't an ex at all. A blessing it would be for the ground to open up and swallow Nicky.

The woman was still smiling. "You're here to see Cullen?"

Nicky couldn't very well turn around and leave, as much as she wanted to. She'd thank him for what he had done, get her stuff, and hightail it back to Riverton. But what an idiot she was, thinking he'd had deep feelings for her. And letting herself fall for him, wanting him more than anything she'd ever wanted in her life. No wonder he hadn't called.

"I'm Marlee," the woman said when Nicky introduced herself. "Come in."

She took a deep breath and stepped into the house.

Cullen was sitting on the sofa in the living room. He looked up as she entered, gave her a small smile. His arm was bandaged and in a sling. He looked pale and his hair was messy as heck, which totally worked for him.

Marlee sat down beside him on the sofa, patted his knee.

Standing in the doorway, Nicky lost her nerve. "I can come back later," she said.

Marlee stood. "Please, don't. I'm sure you have things to talk about and I have an appointment." She leaned down and kissed Cullen on the cheek, then took another glance at Nicky. "It was very nice to meet you." She smiled, not in the least uncomfortable.

When she heard the back door close, Nicky sat down in a chair on the other side of the coffee table, across from the sofa. Cullen looked at her, his lips pinched.

Oh, no.

He said, "How are you?"

Flight and fight were duking it out in her head. One part of her wanted to run, the other to hit him. She sat on her hands, gritted her teeth. "I wasn't the one who was shot. How are you?"

"I'm fine. I'll be back to regular things in no time." A pained expression crossed his face. "I'm sorry about your father. I mean, James Bosko."

"I'll have to get more DNA tests to confirm who my father really is, but he was probably telling the truth." She cleared her throat. "I wanted to ask you what happened, with Karina, I mean. You were standing in front of me so I didn't see. Did she aim for you and miss?"

"It happened pretty quickly, but no, she didn't miss. She hit the target she was aiming for. Have you talked to her?"

"Just for a few minutes this morning. She's under guard at a psychiatric hospital. She seemed okay, just not really that with it. She didn't want to talk about what had happened. She just kept saying how much she hated piano."

Remembering her sister's face that morning, Nicky blinked back tears. She had managed to get out of Karina details about what had happened at the lake all those years ago. To hear Karina tell it, she'd seen Nicky fall and had alerted their mother. It had seemed to carry the ring of truth.

She said, "Will Karina be charged?"

"I don't know. That's not my decision. But maybe not. James Bosko would have killed us, no question about that."

"I feel so bad about that. If I'd realized sooner, we wouldn't have been in that situation."

"He fooled a lot of people. He left zero evidence of the murder. He almost got away with it." He took another sip of water, set the glass on the table. "Have you spoken to your uncle? I mean, your father, if he is your father?"

"I'm still calling him my uncle for now, until it's confirmed. We spoke on the phone at lunchtime. He feels awful. He had no idea my mother and I were in danger. I haven't told him he might be my father."

"It's a lot to get through. It must seem quite overwhelming."

Suddenly, a gush of sadness engulfed her. She'd never felt more alone. Biting back tears, she stood up, walked to the window. After a moment, she said, "We're going to get together tomorrow for lunch in a couple of days. I'll talk to him about that, and I have a lot of questions about his relationship with my mother. I have a feeling his wife knew about the affair. Maybe it broke up their marriage."

"Do you want me to come with you?"

She turned from the window to look at him. "That's okay. I can manage."

He watched her face carefully, concern in his eyes. "I know you can *manage*."

She didn't say anything to that, and for a moment they just stared at each other. But she didn't want his pity, his help, and so she changed the subject. "I'm just still having trouble getting my head around everything. Like, if James Bosko was so angry about the affair, why did he kill my mother and not his brother? Clearly, it wasn't love for his brother that stopped him. I don't think he loved anybody."

"Maybe he knew it was like a slow death, your uncle living

without your mother. The affair was over, but I'm sure Steve still felt deeply for her. They had meant to be married, but James stole her away."

Crossing her arms, she looked out the window again. It was safer than looking at Cullen, whose every glance made her heart squeeze.

She said, "I wonder if he even loved my mother, or if he just married her to spite my uncle. It's all so hard to believe. I knew he wasn't the easiest father, but I thought he loved me. Now I know he hated both of us."

"It's quite possible he didn't care for anybody but himself. Maybe for Karina, but in a twisted sort of way. She was somebody he could control. He fooled his brother, too. His brother swore up and down that he would never have hurt your mother. That James loved her."

She nodded. "I think he wanted to torment his brother. A lot of things that happened make sense now. When we first found out Mom had been murdered, Karina told me not to tell Uncle Steve, that our dad wanted to tell him himself. He must have gotten some kind of sick enjoyment out of that. It was the same thing with making Uncle Steve believe he'd have to speak at the memorial service. Tormenting his brother brought him pleasure."

Cullen stood up, joined her at the window. "You know, sometimes when people are so good at pretending to be one type of person—the caring father and doctor, the grieving husband—it makes it that much easier to be someone else entirely."

She thought about it. "The image he presented of himself

was so real it was hard to see that he was the extreme opposite. A very nasty person."

Cullen's gaze was stark. "You're free of him now."

She nodded. Strangely, talking to Cullen about what had happened was making her feel better. She said, "And Karina's free. She must feel awful for helping with his alibi. She may have known it was Tuesday that she'd last seen Mom, but he tricked her by getting her to change the day to Wednesday. I think she forgot all about that until yesterday. And of course I was too young to realize exactly which day it had been."

"He had it very well planned. The note gave him a few days."

"Do you think he made her write it?"

"He must have."

Nicky went and sat back in her chair, leaving Cullen at the window. James Bosko had obviously lured his wife out to the old farmhouse with the intent of killing her. That thought had consumed her mind for the past day.

He said, "It looks like Allan Spidell committed suicide. The ruling isn't final yet, but there's no sign it was anything other than suicide. He'd had an argument with his wife, who threatened to leave him."

"I realized this morning he'd told me something important when I went to see him at his farm. He said my mother, when they were friends in high school, had her heart set on somebody, but then my dad stole her away. He must have meant my uncle. I wish I'd picked up on it."

He sat down on the coffee table in front of her, leaned forward, and clasped his hands together. "There's something I wanted to talk to you about, something more personal." His expression was serious, almost grim. "I know my timing isn't so great, but I wanted to get it out there."

Heat rising in her cheeks, she looked down. He was getting back with his girlfriend. "I'd rather not discuss it, if you don't mind." She stood up quickly, bumping into his knees, walked across the room to the hallway, turned to look at him. "I just came to say thank you and pick up my things."

He stood up, walked toward her. "Would you let me finish? My ex-girlfriend, Marlee, the woman who was here earlier, she wants to get back together."

A painful tightness thickened her throat. "Oh? She seems nice." Biting her lips to keep from crying, she started up the stairs.

He said, "Where are you going?"

Stopping, she kept a hand on the banister and looked up the stairs, avoiding his eyes. "Upstairs, to get my things." She'd quit her job, move to another town. Maybe another state. California.

He said, "Why can't you leave that stuff here?"

Turning to look at him, she tried to read his face. "What are you talking about? Aren't you getting back together with your girlfriend?" She made her voice sound cold and disinterested.

His answer was a snort. "God, no, not in this life."

A hard knot in her gut that she hadn't realized was there loosened. "Why not?"

"She can't stand the smell of manure. You're the only woman I've met who likes the smell of manure."

She rolled her eyes but her heart was beating faster. "Don't get carried away. I can *tolerate* the smell of manure. Sometimes. In small amounts."

"That's all I ask."

She cocked her brow, still not quite believing what she was hearing. Her head was spinning. "I don't want to be involved in some weird threesome. Does Marlee know it's over?"

He nodded. "She does. She's having a hard time deciding what she wants. A few days ago she wanted to get back together, but now she has her eye on a producer at the station. I'm really not into those kinds of games."

Her heart doing flip-flops now, she walked back down the stairs, stood in front of him. His eyes were so blue, so incredible. The most beautiful eyes in the world.

It took a minute for her to find her voice. "I was wondering why she was friendly to me. She must have really gotten over you quickly."

"A little bit too quickly, if you ask me. But there was another reason for her being so friendly to you."

Her eyebrows shot up. "What's that?"

"She wants to interview you. She tried to persuade me to talk you into it. Your story is very compelling, apparently." He grimaced. "She doesn't even know the half of it."

"Not on your life. The next thing you know I'd be on a reality TV show, earning millions, and injecting myself with Botox."

"The millions would be okay, not the Botox. Anyway, I'm sure she'll find another victim. Apparently, there's a woman who's suing her son because he flunked three courses in his first year of high school."

Nicky clutched her hand to her chest, feigning sadness. "That's a heartbreaking story. If I were a reporter I'd be all over it."

"She seems to think so." He shot her a tentative smile. "So what do you think?"

She was still on the fourth step of the stairs. "Think about what?"

"About you and me. Are you going to break my heart, or do you think we can make it work?"

She looked at him shyly. "Why didn't you call?"

"I didn't know what was going on in your head. You had a lot to process and I didn't want to put pressure on you, push you away. I was giving it until tomorrow." He looked up at her intently. "Come here."

Her cheeks warming, she walked down the stairs until she was on the first step, about the same height as him. He put his good arm round her, pulled her close, and kissed the tip of her nose, then her forehead, cheek, and neck.

Pulling back, he said, "I love you, Nicole." His eyes were serious. "I want to be with you forever."

She whispered, "I love you, too."

There was a sparkle in his eyes. "We'll definitely fight a lot."

She nodded. "I tend to be a lot of trouble."

He stroked her cheek. "I wouldn't have it any other way."

"One other thing," she whispered. "Call me Nicky, will you? My mother always called me that."

He smiled. "I've always wanted to, Nicky Bosko. I just wasn't sure you liked me enough."

"Oh, I like you well enough, Cullen Fraser." A flush spread over her body. She wanted him so badly she was shaking. "Now, let's stop talking."

Putting her arm around his neck, she pulled him close to her, as tight as the sling would allow, and kissed him, hard.

Please see the next page for an excerpt from the first book in Alex Kingwell's Chasing Justice series, EXTREME EXPOSURE!

CHAPTER ONE

Emily Blackstock spotted the first gunman as she was about to make coffee. It was just after five, well before sunrise. Pale moonlight washed the inky night with enough light to see across the rocky ground to the end of the long lane. A pine tree, battered by Atlantic winds, marked the entry to the road.

The man stepped out of the shadows behind the spindly tree.

Emily gave a small start. She dropped the coffee carafe onto the counter, and it fell into the sink with a loud crash.

Oh, God. Please don't let him hear.

She jerked back from the open window, thankful she hadn't turned on the kitchen light, then leaned forward to steal another look. The man gave no sign he'd heard. Tall and burly, he stood facing the old fisherman's cabin, arms held at his sides. His right arm looked several inches longer because of the gun in his hand.

Clutching her arms against her chest, the scene played out

in her mind as a nightmare she'd dreamed every night for weeks. Icy numbness spread to the pit of her stomach. How had they found her? She had been so careful, cut all connections, and even ditched her car. Used only cash. Picked a place to hide so remote it wasn't even a dot on a map.

Trusted no one.

Right now, how didn't matter. They'd found her. And they'd sent someone to kill her.

Not if I can help it.

A glance out the patio doors at the back of the cabin underlined her dismal options. The cabin sat on an island that sloped steeply to the sea. It was surrounded by rocks. No trees for cover. No neighbors. To the front was the road—and those men. To the back, the ocean. Jumping in would be sure death. Those cold, churning waves would swallow her whole.

Up front, the man beside the tree made a beckoning motion with his arm.

She squinted up the road. Two more men, barely in her sight line, climbed out of a dark sedan.

It was all she could do not to scream. Escape one man, maybe. But three? She was as good as dead.

The three men stood in a huddle at the end of the lane. Soon they would come. She couldn't just stand here. She had to try something, move.

Move!

Pulse banging in her throat, she crept around the table and chairs in the cramped dining area. She reached the patio door in seconds, paused to slip on a pair of sneakers, unlocked the sliding glass door, and opened it. She tugged at the screen door, but it refused to budge. Finally, it scraped open. Flinching at the noise, she slipped out, closed both doors. It wouldn't fool them for long, but every second counted.

Standing against the back wall, cold wind lashed her face and whipped her thin shorts against goose-bumped legs. The air smelled damp, briny. Angry waves crashed against the rocks below.

She crossed the small patio, crept down four wooden steps to the ground, then sprinted away from the cabin. Eyes trained on the ground, she jumped recklessly from one wave-washed boulder to another. It was an obstacle course of deep crevices and slippery seaweed.

Her heart beat louder and louder. It had been a mistake to think the cabin was safe. But what else could she have done? They had found her in town, almost killed her.

Tears blinding her, she ran on, landed on a large boulder. Rough rock scraped her bare arms and legs as she slid down on her backside to the rock below. Glancing back, it was too low to see the cabin or any of the men. They were coming, though, and it was getting lighter out. Her eyes darted over the rocks, seeking a place to hide. There was nothing. It would soon be daylight. They'd find her.

There was only one option. She had to get to the edge of the rocks, find a place to climb down. Try to stay out of the water. The waves would toss her back. Or sweep her out to sea.

Not daring to look behind her, she pressed on. The wind beat against her skin, stinging her, leaving a sticky film. Her lips tasted of salt. She'd never ventured this close to the water before. The rocks were too slippery, the waves too high.

Shouts behind told her she had been spotted. A second later, a sharp pop split the air.

Gasping, she dropped to the ground and crouched behind a small boulder. A bullet hit the rock. Razor-sharp fragments of granite pelted her skin like hot needles.

On her feet again, another bullet whizzed by. The last rock was in front of her. From there, it was a sheer twenty-foot drop into the roaring blackness. Blood chilled in her veins. There was no place to climb down.

Across the channel, down a ways, a man stood on the rocky cliff and looked in her direction. A small boat drifting below came into view in the gray light.

They had a fourth man, in the water and ready to go. If she went in, he would make sure she was dead.

Struggling to control her rising panic, she looked behind her. One of the men chasing her was closing in, maybe twenty steps away. The man looked at her with a steady gaze, nothing in his expression. Holding the gun at his side, he walked closer to get a better shot.

It was over. Instead of panic, she felt oddly detached, like she was floating above the rocks, watching herself. She pictured herself already dead.

Something fired in her brain. She was going to die, but she could at least delay it. No use making things easy for them.

Emily pivoted, stepped over the ledge, and plunged into the sea.

* * *

Matt Herrington stood on the mainland setting up the perfect photo. Thick, dark clouds broke at the horizon to reveal a band of red reflected in the water like fire. In fifteen minutes the sun would be up. Showtime.

Matt peered through the wide-angle lens of the camera. On the right of the frame, a small section of the island just up and across the channel protruded into the water. Black and rugged, it was a striking contrast to the water and sky.

He jerked his head back from the camera. Somebody was running on the rocks on the island. A thin, dark shape silhouetted against the flaming sky.

Right into the middle of his perfect picture.

Hairs rose on his neck. Somebody was in a heck of a hurry. Legs pumping, taking long strides. Arms outstretched for balance. It brought to mind a kid pretending to be an airplane, except this was no game.

Higher up, circles of light bounced off the rocks. Two people—no, three—chased the first person. He snapped a telephoto lens onto the camera. The one being chased was small. He scanned up the rocks, focused on the others. They were bigger. Men.

A sick feeling of dread formed in his gut. What was going on? He couldn't call for help, since there was no cell phone service. Clenching his teeth, he instinctively snapped pictures.

If the kid went into the water, his chances would be dim. The current was running fast, with big waves and treacherous whirlpools that could suck in the strongest swimmer. Danger-ous even for the rowboat.

The kid reached the edge of the rocks, glanced in Matt's di-rection. Short hair. A boy?

The boy turned around as one of the men stepped closer to him. The man was easily twice his size. Father?

Holding his breath, Matt waited for him to offer the boy a hand. Put an end to this drama.

Big Guy reached out an arm. But not to help. He was in a shooting stance.

Fighting a wave of nausea, Matt struggled to breathe as the boy turned, stepped out over the rocks, and jumped into the water.

Big Guy walked to the edge of the rocks, leaned over, and fired into the water.

Matt felt the shock like a punch in the gut. He yelled with impotent rage as the two other men joined Big Guy at the edge of the rocks.

The men looked his way, paused a moment, as if debating their options. They backed away, disappeared up the rocks. Must have thought he was too far away to be a viable target in this wind.

For a moment, he couldn't move but in the next instant his mind cleared. Was the kid alive? Doubtful, but there was always a chance. He had to do something. Get his boat over there. Grabbing his gear, he scrambled down the craggy rock face, hiking boots finding familiar footholds. At the bottom, he untied the line tethering the boat to a boulder near the water's edge, hauled it in, and jumped aboard. The small outboard sputtered to life on the second yank of the starter rope.

Starting out across the channel, he drove the boat crosswise into the current, opened the throttle wide, and clutched the steering stick to avoid getting thrown overboard. If the kid was alive, it was a guessing game where he would surface. But it would be somewhere on the other side, maybe straight ahead if the current carried him down the channel.

The boat thumped over the waves and water slopped in, pooling in the flat bottom. The skiff lifted on a big wave and for a moment he couldn't see anything but a brightening sky. It came down and he had a clear view of the cold gray water again. The sun was up, a yellow beach ball on the horizon and the sky's vivid colors were fading into pink as night turned into day.

Agonizing minutes passed before he made it across the channel. The boat was built for stability, not speed, especially not with a three-horsepower outboard.

"Where are you?" he said through gritted teeth, his chest tightening as his eyes darted over the choppy waves. "Come on. I know you're here."

Two minutes later, he glimpsed something dark in the white froth down the channel. Riding closer, he cut the engine, half stood to get a better look. There was something there. The top of a head, the kid's dark hair.

Relief surged through him, making him light-headed. He made a wide circle with the boat, fighting waves for a half minute before he managed to pull up alongside him. Not a boy, but a girl. She stared at him, wide eyed, thick strands of short hair pasted to a pale face. Her arms flailed in the water.

Cutting the motor, he resisted the urge the dive in. If the boat drifted, they'd both be dead. Snatching a life vest, he leaned as far as he could out of the boat, his thighs digging into the wood rail. Icy water drenched the sleeves of his sweater.

"Grab the life jacket," he yelled, holding on to one end so he could drag her in.

The girl snatched a corner of the life jacket, tried to tug it away. "Leave me alone." The words came out as a moan.

"I'm trying to help you." Realizing he was scaring her even more, he modified his tone. "I'm not going to hurt you." He wanted to wrap his hands around Big Guy's meaty throat, squeeze the life out of him.

She wasn't a girl, but a woman, maybe in her midtwenties. The hair was very dark, maybe black. It was impossible to tell the exact color because it was wet. Her pale face with delicate features gave her an ethereal kind of beauty, adding to an impression she would disappear if he didn't get her out of the water soon.

A heavy wave washed over her. Gasping, she spat out a mouthful of seawater.

He reached out to her. "If you don't get in this boat, you're going to drown, or those men will get you." Big Guy and his crew would know she was alive. Maybe they would be thinking about getting a boat at the resort so they could finish the job.

The woman looked around and long seconds passed before she seemed to realize she had no choice. He could have killed her already if that had been his goal. Holding on to the life jacket, she kicked her feet as he pulled her in.

Kneeling, he grabbed the woman under her arms and dragged her into the boat. Even sopping wet, she was light as a feather, and not tall, either, five inches over five feet at the most. He plopped her down on a bench seat.

Her skin was as white as her T-shirt. She wasn't wearing a bra and the wet, translucent fabric clung to round breasts. She might as well have been naked.

Swallowing, he averted his eyes. Looking at her was a bad idea.

The woman folded her arms across her chest and leaned forward, rocking back and forth. She coughed, lifted her head, and stared at him with the greenest eyes he had ever seen. They were big and wild, the pupils just tiny black dots in the center.

Sitting down, Matt wrapped an arm around her and pulled her close. "I'm not going to hurt you."

She didn't say anything, just squirmed under his embrace. She was trembling, her body trying to warm itself. If she stopped shivering, he would worry. Even in August the Atlantic could induce hypothermia.

Rubbing her arm, his hand accidentally brushed the soft curve of a breast. His body responded with a jolt, like a hot signal firing down a wire.

Touching her was a bad idea.

Releasing her, he took off his sweater and handed it to her. She stepped over the seat and sat at the front of the boat, facing him. She had delicate features, soft lips, an upturned nose, and a small chin. But it was those luminous eyes that made him want to grab a camera.

Those eyes measured him as she pulled on the sweater.

"Who are you? What were you doing on the rocks?"

"Taking photos."

She narrowed her eyes. "What kind of photographer takes pictures at night?"

"Not night, twilight. I was there for the sunrise." He turned around to start the boat's motor, glanced back at her. "I should be asking the questions. But right now we need to get the hell out of here."

She looked at him warily, as if she was still deciding whether to trust him. It didn't look like things were going his way. "Where are you taking me?" She yelled to be heard over the noise of the engine and the waves.

"My campsite, a couple of miles down the coast, on the mainland. I have clothes there, and a car."

"Why don't we just go back to where you climbed down?"

"It's farther and it'd be against the tide. Plus, it's just barrens up there. Nothing for miles around. I just stopped in to take some pictures."

The woman tightened her arms across her chest. "I can't let you get involved in this."

Matt scoffed. "What do you want me to do, throw you back in? Pretend I never saw you?"

She didn't say anything, just sat with her body rigid, staring at him. The sweater dwarfed her small, delicate frame, hanging well past her thighs, making her look vulnerable, though there was intelligence and a spark in those electric eyes that told him she was a fighter.

The eyes told him something else. Something about her looks wasn't quite right. Her eyes didn't match the dark hair.

She'd done a dye job with the darkest color she could get her hands on. Her hair would naturally be much lighter, maybe blond, and the haircut was choppy, like she'd done it herself. In a big hurry. A shiver ran down his back. What the hell was she involved in?

Back on the mainland side now, halfway down the channel, they moved quickly with the current. There weren't any other boats in sight.

He decided a couple of questions couldn't wait. "I'm Matt. What's your name?"

"Emily."

"Okay, Emily, who's after you?"

She didn't say anything more for a moment, as if she was considering what to disclose. "I don't know who they are. All I know is they killed my cousin and they tried to kill me." She looked out at the water a moment before meeting his eyes again. "Now they'll kill you."

"I don't intend to get killed and I don't want you to get killed either. The more you tell me, the better off we'll be."

"Just put me ashore at the closest place you can. I can take care of myself."

He let out a snort. "Are you kidding? Those guys are serious." She was in way over her head, and either didn't know it or was too stubborn to accept help. A recipe for disaster.

"You don't think I know that?" Her eyes darkened. "I know it better than anybody. But your part in this ends as soon as you put me on shore."

Shaking his head, he said, "My part in this doesn't end until I deliver you to the nearest police station."

The look she gave him was pure terror. His heart squeezed, as if someone had reached in and twisted it. He tried for a reassuring smile, but there was a sour taste in his mouth. Scared of the police? What the hell? He had a bad feeling about this.

In the next instant that feeling went from bad to worse.

At the end of the channel, a boat appeared as a dot on the water. It could have been a sport fishing boat, of course, chartered at the island resort by a group with nothing more than striped bass on their minds.

But this wasn't a fishing boat. It was headed for them; he'd bet his life on it.

About the Author

An award-winning writer of romantic suspense, Alex Kingwell is a former newspaper reporter, columnist, and editor who much prefers spending her days making stories up. When she's not writing or stuck with her head in a book, Alex can be found running with her dog, obsessing over tribal textiles, or watching offbeat movies with her husband (not necessarily in that order). She lives on the Canadian Prairies.

Learn more at:
AlexKingwell.com
Facebook.com/AlexKingwellBooks
Twitter: @AlexKingwell

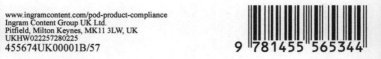